Enlarged Hearts

short stories by

Kathie Giorgio

Mint Hill Books
Main Street Rag Publishing Company
Charlotte, North Carolina

Copyright © 2012 Kathie Giorgio

Cover art: Christopher Werkman
Author photo by Ron Wimmer of Wimmer Photography

Acknowledgments:

Alimentum, The Literature of Food, literary journal:
  "The Fat Girl Inside"
Dos Passos Review: "The Fat Girl Outside"
Women Writers (www.womenwriters.net): "The Fat Girl Goes Steady"

"The Fat Girl Outside" also appeared as a chapter in *The Home For Wayward Clocks* (Main Street Rag, 2011)

Library of Congress Control Number: 2011942433

ISBN: 978-1-59948-336-8

Produced in the United States of America

Main Street Rag
PO Box 690100
Charlotte, NC 28227
www.MainStreetRag.com

A note from the author...

This book is dedicated to my husband, Michael, and my children, Christopher, Andy, Katie and Olivia, for their continued love and support. I have to especially give a nod to Olivia, the only one still at home, who, at eleven years of age, has learned to expect a "Not now, hon, I'm writing," or a "Not now, hon, I'm teaching/reading/editing," response to all of her questions and desires. Of course, this has led to her already writing her own stories and poems, and this makes me happy. I'm not a cupcake-baking mom, and she's okay with that, even on days when I'm not.

A very genuine hug belongs solely to my best friend, Christopher Werkman, who read *Enlarged Hearts* and then somehow created this cover. It is so beautiful.

To everyone at AllWriters' Workplace & Workshop. It's so nice to come equipped with a fan base, batch of groupies, and all-around cheering section. You are all at once my job and my life. Thank you for letting me be a part of your own creative processes.

And of course, a larger-than-life thank you to M. Scott Douglass of the Main Street Rag Publishing Company. You've had faith in me twice now. That means more than you'll ever know.

Love to everyone.

CONTENTS

From Gravity, We Are Free 1

The Fat Girl's Island 4

The Fat Girl Without Jack Sprat. 14

The Fat Girl in Disguise 28

The Fat Girl's Sacrifice 39

The Fat Girl's Glorious Butterball. 47

The Fat Girl Goes Steady. 58

The Fat Girl at the Fair 69

The Fat Girl Inside 84

The Fat Girl Outside 91

The Fat Girl Strides High 100

Being the Fat Girl's Mother 113

The Fat Girl Takes the Long Way 123

The Fat Girl Gives Good Cushion. 134

The Fat Girl and the Seven Bowls. 141

God, Adam, Eve, and Woman,

    as Told by the Fat Girl 182

*Hold on, the weight of the world
will give you the strength to go.*

Linkin Park,
"Robot Boy" from the album, *A Thousand Suns*

FROM GRAVITY, WE ARE FREE

The Fat Girl Proclamation

We walk as land, as a solid, living earthquake. All of us Fat Girls. We roil and we undulate and we steam. If you look close, you see mountains. If you look closer, you see volcanoes of smolder and depth and flame.

There is an extra layer of Woman upon us. Woman, at all of her best. Sensuality is skin upon skin and we are everlasting skin upon skin. Neck to breasts to stomach to thighs, calves, ankles…everywhere, skin touching, moving, constant exorbitant embrace. We are an ocean, rolling ceaselessly over ourselves, rolling ceaselessly over you.

We are inch upon inch, foot upon foot of high-tempered nerve-endings, hypersensitive, mega-aware. Every touch is magnified. Every touch we give is fully loaded.

And we are everywhere. You see us sitting on a subway or a park bench, or walking slowly down the street, appearing to sink into the ground with every step. You see us as sad, as having one foot, one knee, one thigh in the grave. Our bodies our coffin. For some of us, that's true. If a Fat Girl is still shrinking from human reprimand, if she is still shying away from her own depths, then she is sad. How hard to be so large and feel so small at the same time! How could such richness be worthless? Why should we want to be shallow? Sheer excess makes us alive and life-seeking and free. We dive into ourselves and then rejoice out, making thin air thick with life and soul and spirit. We are not sinking. We are savoring. There is an extra layer of Woman upon us.

We know how to relish, and we do. We enjoy all that is offered and earthy and real. We feel every motion through our bodies, and those motions are delicious. The earth is at our feet and the sky is above our heads, and the ocean beats our hearts enlarged. From gravity, we are free.

When we are accompanied, we are with those who appreciate us. They understand that the heft of our breasts, each lifted and celebrated in two hands, comes from more than hunger. It comes from desire, the desire to know it all, to feel it all, to embrace and take in and expand. It comes from joy.

Have you heard us sing? Have you heard the full voices that swoop out of full bodies, that climb scales, fall back, and soar again, through stanzas and staffs and serenades? Voices that flood a room, stream over your shoulders, overflow your pores. The voice of Woman. The voice of pure joy. Satisfaction.

We have an extra layer of Woman upon us.

Fat Girls recognize each other from across the room. We recognize each other from across the continent. We pass each other and we nod and we know. Our smiles are for us alone.

Can you imagine us all together? Arm in arm, flesh to flesh, under a moon that is one glorious curve. One full circle, a reflection of all that is light and dark and grounded and floating. The moon calls us out, with the chill of the air, and we meet amid songs and exhibition. Our skin glows silver, our hair flows free, and there is a path to the sky and to us. A connection of skin and silk and silver and curves and glory and larger than life. On earth, we are the moon. And in the sky, the moon is us. Round and fulfilled.

Enlarged Hearts

From gravity, we are free.

Moon-soaked, we raise our faces and we sing. All those voices soar from all those bodies, rustle trees, wave ocean, spark sky. Round faces atop round bodies, round mouths inundating melody, harmony, round hands slapping round knees in rhythm. All of us rejoicing. We are Rejoice.

We are alive. Everything in us is bounty and burgeon. We are full, we are large, we are lovely. When you look at us, you should never see death. Never a foot in a grave, never a body as a coffin. Just life, life in curve upon curve, in mountain cresting mountain, life in our touch, our song, our connection to the earth and the sea and the moon.

We are the Fat Girls. We have an extra layer of Woman upon us. We are Woman. And from gravity, we are free.

THE FAT GIRL'S ISLAND

Every morning at 9:35, as she prepared her store for opening, the Fat Girl watched the Gilligan Twins stride by. Well, the Twins used to stride. Thirty-three years ago, when the Fat Girl first started at the Large & Luscious Large Women's Clothing Boutique in the mall, the Twins strode, then time smoothed them to a walk, and now a stroll, one with the use of a cane. They used to circle the mall four times, but gradually, the rotations decreased and now they were down to just one circuit. On the Fat Girl's very first day at Large & Luscious, she looked up from training at the digital screen cash register just as the floppy white hats passed by. She didn't know for sure that the Twins started on the exact same morning she did, but it felt fortuitous to see them on that first day of full-time work when she was twenty-two years old, nine months post-partum from college, and couldn't find another job anywhere because of her size.

She'd interviewed at least fifty different times, trying to hide her bulk in a suit bought right there at Large & Luscious. But despite the black sleek and professional fabric, her hips still bulged out beneath the armrests of every interviewing chair. Her degree in English wasn't going to get her very far anyway, and no one ever told her she was too fat for the job, but the Fat Girl knew better. She knew what the short Q & A times meant, she knew what the employers were really saying when their questions became cryptic and they didn't even write down her answers. When they wouldn't meet her eyes. When they shook her hand and said, "We'll let you know," and then they never did. She returned to Large & Luscious that day thirty-three years ago in search of a more magical suit, in a more slimming color, or with just a slightly different cut, but she found a magic sign instead. Help Wanted. Her organized attitude and gentle, yet firm manner caught Corporate's attention. The Fat Girl was fifty-five years old now and she'd risen to the top level of store manager fifteen years ago.

The Gilligan Twins were men and the Fat Girl named them herself for their hats, unfolded, floppy-brim sailor hats that reminded her of Gilligan from the old television series, Gilligan's Island. They wore the hats every single day, no matter the weather, no matter the season. The Fat Girl was stunned once when one of the men happened to pull off his hat to wipe his brow just as he was passing the store and she got a glimpse of his round bald head. Somehow, she expected crisp brown hair. Maybe even tight curls. But no, this Twin sported shiny skin, and so she assumed the other did as well. The Twins were spitting images of each other and wore identical clothing, except for the colors. One Twin preferred red, the other blue. In the summer, they wore khaki cargo shorts and one Twin wore a red wifebeater and the other a blue one. In the winter, they wore old man baggy jeans and a red sweatshirt and a blue sweatshirt. Always the hats. Always white socks and white sneakers. They seemed to reserve the sneakers only for walking in the mall; the shoes were never dirty. They moved through their circuit with an identical gait, left legs, right legs, left legs, right legs. Their faces were turned toward each other and they were always talking. The Fat Girl wondered what it was that they still had to say to each other, after so many years; the Fat Girl placed the Twins in their seventies. Now that the Red Twin walked with a cane, the Blue Twin swung his arm out like his brother and held his hand palm downward as if he held a cane too.

The Fat Girl was the longest-lasting employee at Large & Luscious. One girl had been there for twenty-five years, celebrated recently with goblets of white sangria at Applebee's after nine o'clock. But while the Fat Girl and this particular co-worker talked and joked a lot, having known each other for a couple decades, they talked and joked only within the confines of Large & Luscious. When they worked the same shift, they said goodbye and then walked to their respective cars and drove to their respective homes. It was the same with all of the co-workers at Large & Luscious. Even though the Fat Girl never said a word to the Gilligan Twins, she still felt closer to them, raising the same hand, her right hand, every day to the Twins as they walked by. Sometimes, they waved back. Other times, they were too engrossed in their conversation. But regardless, they'd been there with the Fat Girl since day one and no one else had been.

Then Corporate told her she didn't have to open and close the store every day. "You're the manager," Corporate said. "You've been the manager for fifteen years and you've done a great job. You're one of the highest-profit stores that we have. Give yourself a break. Let yourself sleep in, work late morning to the early evening, be home in time for supper. We appreciate your loyalty and dedication, but it's time to let someone else do the open and close. You're getting up there in years, you know. Retirement age. We don't want you to be too stressed-out. We want you to keep your store at top level. So be a good manager and delegate."

The Fat Girl thought about this. Ever since she'd become manager, she'd been there at opening and she'd been there at closing, even though she was only paid for eight hours a day. It was her store, after all, her baby, and she just felt that she should be there, the way a mother wants to be the first her baby sees when those eyes open in the morning, and the last when they close at night. The Fat Girl at least gave herself the weekends off, and the only holiday she worked was Black Friday, when everyone worked. But now, at fifty-five, the Fat Girl wondered what it might be like to eat supper at six o'clock, a supper that she actually cooked herself from fresh ingredients, from recipes garnered from cookbooks collected over the years from the clearance bins at the mall's bookstore. Having a cup of coffee with her dessert because it wouldn't be so late that it would keep her up. A glass of wine before bed. Spending more than a couple hours in lounge clothes. She imagined sitting on her couch and actually watching the shows that everyone else talked about. Maybe some nights, she could actually use the bathtub in her apartment. Candles. Scented bubbles. Just like in the commercials that the Fat Girl rarely saw. Though to be truthful, the Fat Girl wasn't sure if she'd even fit in her bathtub. She'd only taken showers for years.

So maybe she could give up her evenings at the store. The Fat Girl could trust the others to close the shop, balance the cash registers, even make the deposit. For sure, the co-worker who'd been there for twenty-five years could be trusted with the deposit. Really, they all could. They were nice responsible women.

But the mornings. The Gilligan Twins. Who would wave to them? Who would wave to the Fat Girl?

At 9:35 the next morning, the Fat Girl watched the heads bob by. The Twins both answered her wave. And then she called to the sales clerk in the back, bringing out a new armload of pink Large & Luscious shopping bags. "Can you take over opening?" the Fat Girl asked. "I'll be back in a bit."

The other fat girl looked dumbfounded, but quickly agreed. As the Fat Girl knew she would. You didn't say no to the manager, after all.

Nudging her way through the sliding glass doors, the Fat Girl trundled after the Gilligan Twins. There were five other walkers between them, an older couple and three singles, but the Fat Girl could easily see the white hats dipping in front of her. Two of the singles were elderly and walked with walkers cushioned with green tennis balls and the Fat Girl passed them handily. The couple stopped to check out a store display and the Fat Girl moved by them as they checked their pulses. But the third single wasn't young, and she wasn't old either and she walked with free weights and she seemed determined to maintain her space directly behind the boys. There was no room to pass her unless the Fat Girl passed the Gilligan Twins too, and she didn't want to do that. Still, even from this distance, she thought she caught the tones of their Twin voices from time to time. Rumbled words, even the short bark of laughter. Near parking lot B, they swung off down the side entrance hall and the Fat Girl stood there, panting, and watched them go through the automatic doors into the morning sunlight. She wondered what kind of car they owned. She wondered who drove. Blue, probably. The Twin without the cane.

On the way back to the store, walking more slowly, the Fat Girl decided it was indeed time to delegate. She wouldn't open the store in the morning. Instead, she would come in and chase the Gilligan Twins. She would find out what it was they had to talk about. She would find out why they were so close.

The next morning, the Fat Girl walked into the mall, not with the other workers, but with the other walkers. She sported a bright pink velour jogging suit, bought at Large & Luscious with her employee discount, and new white walking sneakers from Athlete's Foot. Waiting at the end of Entrance B, she pretended she knew what she was doing and stretched against the wall while watching for the bobbing heads of the Gilligan Twins. Upstairs, at Large & Luscious, the Fat Girl hoped the twenty-five year co-worker was successfully opening the store. The Fat Girl felt out of place, stretching there. She was supposed to be counting out the money in the cash registers right now, then making sure all the clothes were arranged properly, according to size and style and color, then double-checking the floors for any loose threads, buttons or ripped-off pricetags. For a moment, she felt disoriented, dizzy, and she thought about making a dash for her store, telling the twenty-five year fat girl that she changed her mind, and settling back into her usual routine.

But then the Gilligan Twins walked in, their heads together, already in conversation. The Fat Girl waited until they passed, then she fell in behind them. Their pace was brisk, at least for the Fat Girl, and she concentrated on watching their legs. Left, right, left, right. Carefully, she matched her steps to theirs and listened as her thighs settled into a swish-swish rhythm, providing harmony with the slip-slide percussion of their cargo shorts. The Fat Girl liked it; she caught herself smiling, nodding to the beat. To their beat, the Twins and her own. Their heads nodded too, and she caught the accompaniment of their voices. She didn't know what they said, but it didn't matter. All that mattered was that she moved with them in this circuit, left, right, left, right, swish-swish, slip-slide, and her arms and legs and hips and head moved within the company of others. In sync. In touch.

By the end of the circuit, the Fat Girl was swathed in sweat, the pink velour matted into a crimson. Back at Entrance B, she stood and swayed gently, waiting for her heart rate to slow, and watched the boys step toward the door. During their walk, they never once turned toward her, but she still felt acknowledged in their presence. They hadn't sped up; they hadn't slowed down. They stayed with her the whole time. And now, right before they went through the automatic doors, they looked back, and each one raised a right hand in a wave. She waved back.

The change in rhythm and routine rippled through the Fat Girl's life like a shudder of pleasure. The morning walks led to lighter discussions at work, commiserations over weight, home details shared, asking the twenty-five year co-worker to take an afternoon break with her at Starbucks, laughter over lattes. Followed by different breaks, different co-workers, sandwiches and cups of soup at lunch. Then came the dinners at home, lessons learned from the cookbooks, shared recipes, meals actually set out on the table on pretty plates, accompanied by silverware and a tall glass of wine, gourmet coffee with dessert. Weeks passed and after the dishes were cleared, there was the nightly entertainment of television shows, dramas, comedies, laughter and tears and the wondering of what would happen next. And then a phone call from another fat girl who was watching the same thing. A discussion. Finally, evenings at this fat girl's house or that one's, a community of co-workers not at work munching TV treats and dissecting storylines. At night, bed, with the anticipation of knowing that the next morning, it all started over again. With a walk in a pink velour jogging suit whose inner thighs were rubbed smooth and that was quickly growing too large.

Eight months in, summer gone, winter entrenched in white snow and gray skies, the Fat Girl stretched by Entrance B one morning, pacing in place and waiting for the Gilligan Twins. Other walkers who recognized her now had already moved on and she glanced at her watch and worried. When it got to be a half-hour late, the Fat Girl gave up and swung out on her own.

But her rhythm was marred. She tried to keep the beat, to picture the boys in front of her, to slide into the rhythm she thought she knew so well. But she wasn't sure if she was going too fast or too slow and so she sped up or idled down and her feet felt too big for her body. Her jogging suit made a new sound now, not a swish-swish, but a swampy slop-over of too much material. She promised herself that during lulls at work, she would look at different suits, would buy one in a smaller size. She, the Fat Girl, was smaller, though today, she felt the smallest of all. She felt all by herself, out there in the mall. Some people passed her and waved, but it wasn't the same as jiving to the Gilligan Twins' beat. No one stayed with her. She waved at her co-workers as she passed by the store and they gestured and pointed and she shrugged. I don't know where they are, she thought. I don't know. I don't even know their names. They're just Red and Blue. They're just the Gilligan Twins.

The Fat Girl finished her walk, feeling disappointed. But that afternoon, she picked out another jogging suit, two sizes smaller, in a gentle soft meadow green. When she tried it on, she felt like she shimmered.

The rest of the week passed, and there were no Gilligan Twins. Sad, the Fat Girl drove home for the weekend. She watched television and cooked and relaxed on the couch. She drove out to the lakefront and walked along the frozen beach and wondered how Lake Michigan compared to the ocean. She sat on a rock and watched the stars come out, mixing in a haze with the steam of the city and her own warming breath. A co-worker, a friend, called her cell phone and the Fat Girl talked to her and listened as the rise and fall of the friend's voice blended with the waves of the great lake. She closed her eyes and felt the rhythm and rocked to it.

On Sunday, she met some of the other fat girls for brunch and then they sat around her apartment and watched a football game that none of them understood, but it didn't matter. They talked. They rubbed elbows. They hugged and touched and patted and the Fat Girl nodded and fell in with it. She was still sad, but there were voices here in her home, and arms that lifted her up. When she went to bed that night, she looked forward to the next day. She hoped the Gilligan Twins would return in the morning. She pictured one, Red, with a rolling gravel cough; she pictured the walk as slower, but the slow didn't stop the rhythm and it set in and healed like hot deli soup in a favorite chipped mug.

But when the Fat Girl waited by Entrance B, and the automatic doors swung open, only one Twin walked in. At first, the Fat Girl wasn't sure who he was. He didn't wear red and he didn't wear blue. He wore a purple sweatshirt. He passed her and the Fat Girl watched, and then she realized. He didn't have a cane. And he walked on the outside track, closest to the stores. It was Blue. Blue without Red.

Maintaining her distance, the Fat Girl followed along. Blue seemed to wander a bit, drifting over what would be the center line. At first, his hand swung out as if he grasped a cane, but then it fisted and just listed back and forth, a lackluster paddle in a doldrum river. He kept his head turned inwards, but the Fat Girl could see that he didn't say a word. His mouth turned down and the lines on his face were deep, engraved with more than age.

When they passed Large & Luscious, the Fat Girl looked in. The twenty-five year co-worker was ready with a wave and the Fat Girl waved back. She thought of all the years of waving at the Gilligan Twins, not saying a word, just waving, and how they waved back, and how she named them, and how they became a part of her life. She thought of their conversation, the way their heads turned toward each other, the even rumble of their words, the discussion that never seemed to have a lull or an end. And she thought of the discussions with her co-workers, her friends now, the fat girls she'd worked with for years and used to pass only pleasantries with. How now they talked. How they made no sense sometimes and they giggled, how they made too much sense other times and they sighed. How she went to bed at night thinking about what one fat girl said, what another wore, how a third was losing her mother, a fourth struggling with her health. The Fat Girl thought of the rubbing elbows, the nodding heads. And the wave, that wave every morning, no matter who was at the cash register. She thought how she knew every fat girl behind the cash register, and now she knew them away from it too.

The Fat Girl looked ahead at Blue, saw him tilt toward the center, veer back to the right. She picked up her pace, snugged herself shimmering beside him, slid her arm through his. "Hi," she said.

Blue looked at her. "Hi," he said back. She saw that true to his name, he had blue eyes. And that they shimmered with tears. At first, the Fat Girl didn't know what to say. At first, she thought about dropping back. But then she felt his hand tighten on her arm.

She told him her name. He nodded and offered his own. His tone was soft and she felt the rumble, as familiar and steady as the waves of Lake Michigan. As familiar and steady as her friend's voice on the phone.

They turned their heads together and fell into a nod and the Fat Girl synced their steps. Left, right, left, right. She kept her arm firmly wrapped in his. She felt her own tears. "It'll be all right," she said.

Close together, they continued their circuit. His name wasn't Blue. And hers wasn't the Fat Girl.

THE FAT GIRL WITHOUT JACK SPRAT

Jack Sprat could eat no fat,
His wife could eat no lean,
And so between them both, you see,
They licked the platter clean.

The Fat Girl knew she was truly alone when she couldn't reach her photo albums. Her husband always retrieved them for her. Jack had been terrified of fire, and he insisted on putting the photo albums on the top shelf of the kitchen cabinet furthest from the stove, believing that they were safest there, the flames weren't likely to lick that high. The Fat Girl couldn't reach the upper shelves of any of the cabinets, she was too short, which was why Jack always retrieved them for her. Their marriage was like that.

The Fat Girl originally fell in love with Jack because of his name. His whole body reflected Spratness. His last name wasn't really Sprat, but he was Jack, a tall skinny man with a light dusting of brown hair when they met, and a totally bald head when he died. They laughed at the incongruity of their sizes, the nursery rhyme of their joining. When the Fat Girl made love with her skinny man, when in later years, she kissed his bald head as he nestled between her breasts, she was incredibly lucky, incredibly blessed, and incredibly happy. And she knew it.

When Jack died, they both weren't young, so death wasn't completely unexpected. But the fact that Jack went first, and from a heart attack, was. Jack remained skinny all of his life. He ate well, following carefully the changes in the food pyramid as different theories were discovered and others discarded and then recovered again. For most of his life, he was a long distance runner. In their early and middle years, the Fat Girl would come down to breakfast just as Jack was lacing up his sneakers. She kissed him out the door, and then made herself a full breakfast, eggs, bacon, toast, juice, coffee, afterwards placing her dishes in the dishwasher beside his single juice glass. She showered and dressed for her job at the Large & Luscious Large Women's Clothing Boutique in the mall, then pretended to dig through the refrigerator for fixings for her lunch. She always opted for the food court instead, but she felt she owed it to Jack to at least look at the healthy food he bought. Their marriage was like that.

Climbing in her minivan, the Fat Girl would head off down the road, following a special route, and eventually, she caught sight of Jack up ahead, a tall praying mantis in gray and white flapping shorts and a white t-shirt, running away from her. She checked the time and noted if he was right on schedule, a little ahead, or a little behind, then she zipped past him and pulled over. He jogged in place next to her driver's door as she handed out a room temperature bottle of water. He drained it, then stopped running to lean inside, into her arms, and kissed her wetly on the lips. She relished the wet, with the warmth of his mouth just beneath. She could smell him, and that smell lingered on her clothes, in her hair, on the palms of her hands. Pulling away from the curb, she watched him in the rearview mirror, growing smaller and smaller, his hand shooting up rhythmically in a wave, and she blinked her flashers at him just before she crested a hill and he disappeared.

As Jack grew older, he gradually slowed and eventually just walked, though he still did his old route almost every day. The Fat Girl still brought him his water. Right before he died, she fantasized about retirement, a little over a year from then, when instead of driving away, she would wait at home. She would probably sleep until his return, and instead of her bringing him a bottle of water, he would present her with a hot cup of coffee and a kiss. Heat upon warmth.

But it was Jack that fell from a heart attack, dead in less than five seconds, on the side of the road one morning. Jack, who ate vegetables and fruit, who was never an ounce overweight, who never drank a soda in his entire life, neither sugared nor diet. The Fat Girl didn't collapse, her husband did, and she was the one who found him, face down in the gravel. She pulled up behind him instead of ahead of him, and when she fell to her knees on the side of the road, the thump made his body vibrate, just a bit, just enough for her to think he was still alive. But he wasn't and she wailed and it was a while before she had the presence of mind to call 911.

There was all the usual activity around a death. The arranging of the funeral and all its accoutrements. The circling of friends, all the ladies from Large & Luscious, all of Jack's buddies, mixing together like a strange salad of butternut squash and green beans. To be sure, her friends brought the best comfort food, desserts rich in chocolate, casseroles thick with noodles and cream of mushroom soup. Jack's friends brought healthier things, relish trays and fruit platters, as if, the Fat Girl thought, that saved Jack at all in the end. She was given a bereavement leave of two weeks from work, and in that time, she went through all the gift food, except for the relish trays which moldered in the crisper.

The night before the Fat Girl returned to work, she sat in her living room, in her recliner, and glanced from time to time at Jack's empty chair. He'd always preferred a wing-backed easy chair with an ottoman. During the luncheon after the funeral, someone pushed the ottoman up so that it was tight against the chair, rather than giving Jack space to put his legs in between as he sat down or stood up. Ever since, the Fat Girl paused whenever she passed the ottoman, tempted to push it back to its comfortable position, but then resisting.

She hadn't resisted with Jack's sneakers. She'd ridden in the ambulance to the hospital, turning around in the front seat, watching as the paramedics sweated and pounced over Jack's body. In the ER, the doctors only perfunctorily worked on Jack as he was already dead. It was just a few minutes' wait before she was ushered in to view him. The first thing the Fat Girl noticed were his feet dipping over the end of the table. His white shirt was cut open and spread and reddened circles were on his skin from where they suction-cupped electrodes to him to find any hint of a heartbeat. He still wore his gray shorts and his running sneakers. The hospital staff handed her a box of tissues, a cup of coffee and a bottle of water, then left her alone to say her goodbyes. The Fat Girl dropped it all, kissed Jack's cold lips, and laid her head for a long time on his silent and steady chest. Then she carefully unlaced his sneakers, slid them off his feet, and carried them home. She thought they were still warm.

Upstairs, she lined up the sneakers in their bedroom closet, toes pointing in, heels out, just the way Jack did. She sprayed them with FeBreeze, even though she knew that would diminish Jack's running-feet scent. He liked the FeBreeze; he said it allowed him to smell flowers even on snowy days.

During her two weeks bereavement leave, The Fat Girl cried in fits and starts. Every time she found herself in tears, the Fat Girl stopped herself, considered the moment, examined it, and wondered if it was a normal time to cry, a normal way to grieve. She felt her size was already abnormal enough; she didn't want to stick out any more, now that she didn't have Jack's everyday assurances that she was glorious. The Fat Girl heard of other widows crying into their husband's pillows, or sleeping in one of their husband's shirts. The Fat Girl took a shirt straight out of the hamper, but wearing it was out of the question; she wouldn't be able to get both arms in, let alone tug it down over her breasts. So she wrapped it around Jack's pillow, and at night, she wept into them both. During the day, she worked hard at restraining herself. Staying at home helped; there was no one to see if she did break down.

On this night before returning to work, before venturing back out in public, Jack's sneakers were still in his closet, and they were still empty. Lining up the sneakers hadn't brought him back. The FeBreeze hadn't brought him back. And neither would returning the ottoman to its original position. Doing things for Jack wouldn't bring him back. But she still wanted to. Their marriage was like that.

Glancing again at the empty chair, the Fat Girl suddenly felt an urge to look through her photo albums. She didn't think that would be unusual, it seemed like a typical grieving thing to do, and so she heaved herself up and trundled to the kitchen. She opened the cabinet furthest from the stove and looked up at the leatherbound albums, at least a foot past her reach.

Going into the pantry, the Fat Girl found the little wooden footstool that Jack used twice a year to clean the tops of the cabinets, one of the few places in the house that he couldn't reach on his own. She placed it appropriately, then put one foot on top. It seemed sturdy enough, and so she braced her hands on the counter and hoisted herself up. Her free leg wobbled in the air and she swayed precariously. Her thighs were too large, they prevented her from being able to put both feet on the stool at the same time. Holding her breath, she attempted to balance on one foot, sticking one arm out like a divining rod and reaching up with the other. But the footstool began to creak. Quickly, for her, she climbed down.

Weak in the knees, overcome suddenly with sadness, the Fat Girl sat down on the stepstool and the thing gave up and collapsed. Sprawled on the floor, splinters and hurt scattered around her, the Fat Girl gave in for a moment, just a moment, throwing aside considerations of normalcy, and she howled. She couldn't reach the albums. Jack's chair was empty. In bed, there was only his shirted pillow. His sneakers still smelled good. There was no Jack. There was no Jack. There was no Jack.

But then, like a slap, she stopped and concentrated on the matter at hand. It took a while to work herself to her knees, and then from her knees to standing, but she did it. She cleaned up the broken footstool and put it in the trash and closed the cabinet, checking to make sure that the kitchen was tidy again. As clean as Jack liked it. As clean as he kept it.

She went to bed. Tomorrow during her lunch hour, she decided, she would go to Sears and try to find another way to reach the photo albums.

As the Fat Girl pulled out of her garage in the morning, she panicked. She wasn't sure which way she should drive to work. She'd been told over and over at Jack's funeral that the thing to do was to get back to routine as soon as possible. That made sense to her, but routine meant driving Jack's route on the way to the mall. There was another way, a shorter way, that she only used during bad snowy mornings when it was too slippery for Jack to run. So was it normal to take Jack's route, trailing a blinding June sun, even if it meant passing that spot where she found him, and passing that other spot where she typically parked and gave him his water and received her kiss? Or was normal going the way she would have always gone if she'd never had Jack in the first place?

Idling at the end of her driveway, the Fat Girl turned her steering wheel first this way, then that. Facing Jack's route, she was washed in horror over seeing Jack's death spot, a place she'd avoided since the day she found him. Facing the freeway, she was washed in misery, in the sadness of absence, in the now familiar realization that she would never see him again. The realization that came with the ottoman and the waiting sneakers and the photo albums. In the end, she took the freeway, thinking she was most likely then to get to work without tears. But she cried anyway as she headed down the entrance ramp. She had to redo her makeup before going in to the mall.

The ladies at Large & Luscious were subdued in their welcome backs, and the Fat Girl couldn't blame them. How do you treat a co-worker who went home a wife on a Thursday, and came back as a widow two weeks later? She knew the other Fat Girls were happy to see her, but she knew they were also sad for the reason she was gone. The Fat Girl accepted the hugs and she held back her tears and she got to work. She returned to the routine. The other Fat Girls followed her lead, and soon, everything was as normal. Customers, clothing, whispered sizes, laments and diet declarations.

During her break, though, she split from the routine and turned down the offer to eat with other breaking co-workers at the food court. The Fat Girl explained that she had a few errands to run, thank you cards and such, and sure enough, that brought silence and sad nods from the others. With a wave, the Fat Girl turned left and rode down the escalator, and then she walked to Sears.

In the kitchenwares department, the Fat Girl found another stepstool exactly like Jack's. She pondered it for a while, wondering if she should replace it, even though she would never be able to use it.

In another aisle, there was a wonderful retro ladder chair, just like the one that used to be in her mother's kitchen. The Fat Girl wondered where that one went; she always loved the thing, covered with about twenty layers of paint for every time her mother changed the color of the kitchen. This new ladder chair was as tall as a barstool, bright red metal reminiscent of Coca-Cola, and it had two steps that folded out of it, making the chair into a miniature staircase. But again, the width of it, from left to right, wasn't much, no wider than the stepstool, and the Fat Girl knew she would never be able to have both feet upon it at the same level at the same time. So she gave it a fond pat and moved on.

There were no other options in the kitchenwares department, so she walked over to hardware. There, they had ladders of all heights, but width was again the problem. How would she ever be able to balance if she couldn't use both feet? And would the ladders even hold her? The labels cheerfully announced their weight limitations, and while the Fat Girl didn't know exactly how much she weighed (her doctor's scale stopped at three-hundred), she was pretty sure she weighed more. The ladders shaped like an A would place her further from the cabinet, requiring her to lean and stretch over the counter, or she would have to climb and stretch sideways. The other ladders, the traditional ones that were braced against whatever you were supposed to be climbing, scared her. She'd have to have the cabinet door already open; leaning the ladder against shelving seemed dangerous. And her floor was tile, black and white classic that Jack installed just for her on her fiftieth birthday. Tile was slippery. The Fat Girl pictured the ladder sliding, and herself riding it as it fell, bouncing against her countertop and then dropping flat to the floor, her fingers and knees and toes probably breaking.

The Fat Girl sighed and returned to the kitchenwares department. She stopped by the ladder chair again, thinking how nice it would look perched on her black and white tile, how it would pop with color against her white cabinets, her black granite countertop. Her kitchen did look a little like a diner, like a soda fountain, and she could decorate around the chair, with red cups, red plates, a vase with red flowers on the table. For a second, she smiled, but then she remembered her decorum, her station, and her lips went straight again. It was so hard being a new widow. She couldn't be too sad. She couldn't be too happy. The Fat Girl wasn't sure how long these restrictions would last. She only knew that any feelings at this time just weren't appropriate. She was supposed to be in a fog, a life limbo of sorts, holding herself in while her old life transitioned into her new life. She had to be brave. She had to be strong. She turned away from the ladder chair.

Finding herself back at Jack's stepstools, the Fat Girl pulled one from the stack and set it in the middle of an aisle. Then she looked back at the stack again. She could replace the one and buy another, so she could have one stool for each leg. They would act in tandem like a bench. But she worried about stability, about the possibility of one sliding or slipping or if she could possibly kick the second one over as she hefted herself up to the first.

When she went to get another stepstool, she discovered a second stack. There were two different styles; one with a square top, like Jack's, and one with a circle top. She picked up a circle and placed it next to the square. They were identical heights, and identical too in the legs. Studying them, the Fat Girl thought that maybe the round top would decrease her chances of kicking it as she raised her foot. There were no corners to catch with a toe. She wished she could try it out, but in the kitchenwares department, the counters were full of china and glassware.

The Fat Girl liked the way the stepstools looked, the two of them, standing next to each other. Pushing them closer together, she heard the clunk as they collided. They made her think about that old phrase, about the square peg going into a round circle, and she suddenly caught herself smiling again. After glancing around to make sure no one noticed, she decided to bring home the two, the square and the circle, untested. They just looked trustworthy, squatting side by side in the middle of all the breakables.

The Fat Girl placed the stepstools in the pantry when she got home. There wasn't room for them to stand beside each other in there, but she discovered that despite the difference in their tops, their legs allowed them to nest, and so she placed the round one on top of the square, admiring the way it slid down and snugged tight to the other.

Before she'd returned from lunch, she stopped at Barnes & Noble and browsed through the self-help section, a stepstool standing on either side of her like obedient children. There were an alarming number of books on grieving. She finally chose one just based on its title, "Your Grieving Time," because that was exactly what she felt she was in. A grieving time. That soon it would pass and she would return to the normal time. The everyday time. Even though she knew that was impossible because Jack was never going to lace up his sneakers again.

Now, after nestling the stepstools and fixing herself a sandwich and a bowl of soup and some chips, she carried her new book to her recliner. She glanced again at the pushed-tight ottoman. Leaving the television off, she opened her book.

There really wasn't anything there she didn't already know. The book talked about hugging a pillow, smelling a shirt. It talked about the difference between losing someone early in a relationship and losing a lifelong partner. The Fat Girl read those words, lifelong partner, and she read them again and then the words blurred and she was crying as if she'd been crying for hours. There was no welling up, no increasing gasps. She was just in the middle of a storm and she had to fling the book away for fear of soaking the words right off the page.

A lifelong partner. That's just what Jack was. They married when the Fat Girl was twenty-three and now she was sixty. That was a lifetime. But their lifetime was gone because Jack was.

Except the Fat Girl was still here.

When the tears dried, the Fat Girl glanced at the ottoman again and then she got up to go to the kitchen. She retrieved the stepstools and set them, side by side, in front of the cabinet. She checked to see that each of her feet were centered in front of a stool.

But when she looked up, the cabinet seemed so far away and she was suddenly drenched with exhaustion. Even with both stepstools for her balance, she reasoned, she was just too tired to do any more that day. That book said that exhaustion was normal. She was normal. She was so tired.

A cup of tea would do the trick, she decided. Something to soothe her, calm her nerves before going to bed. The Fat Girl would follow exhaustion's prescription and go to bed early, before the late night show she and Jack always watched. It was a break in routine, but one she felt would help her combat this grief time. Sleep would let her hack at grief like a machete, clearing the way through the sucking vines that threatened to pull her apart. In the morning, she hoped there would be a clearing. A fresh green field.

And Jack. He always liked daffodils.

As the Fat Girl sat and drank her tea, delicious accompanied by a few butter cookies, she looked at the two stepstools. They squatted there on their identical legs, both the same color and the same height, but with different tops. The curvy side of the circle and the straight side of the square were just touching, just kissing, and the Fat Girl caught herself smiling again, charmed at her own thoughts. The warmth and the sweet of her treat was getting to her, she thought, and she quickly pursed her lips and looked away. But before she left the kitchen, before she darkened it for the night, the Fat Girl decided to leave the two stepstools out, standing sentinel by the cabinet. She nestled them again, one on top of the other, and she risked one last smile as she shut the lights out.

A few more days went by and the stepstools became a part of a new routine. The Fat Girl would come home from work, un-nestle the stools, set them side by side, then go about her business of preparing a dinner for one. After dinner, she read a little of the grief book, or watched the television or did the crossword puzzle in the paper. Since Jack's passing, she hadn't been able to finish a single one. He always seemed to know what she didn't.

As the time pushed on to nine o'clock, she'd crave seeing the photo albums again. She stood by the counter, concentrating at first on her toes, centering each foot to a stool. She opened the cabinet, stared at the albums, saw the leather, remembered how soft it felt in her hands. She remembered putting the pictures inside, each new roll of film gleefully waited for. She and Jack would sit at the kitchen table, write on the photos' backs, and flatten them onto the sticky thick paper. It was like reliving the event, the two of them recalling details the other didn't, and their laughter blending like milk and chocolate into a pudding. The Fat Girl remembered, and she closed the cabinet, and stepped back. She wondered what she was forgetting.

She was just so tired.

A month and a half to the day since Jack died, six weeks of grief studied and stuffed, the Fat Girl sat at her table with her tea and her cookies and she stared at the cabinet she'd just closed. The stools were still ready, side by side, their wood touching, the square to the circle, their legs lining up just so. The Fat Girl stopped in mid-sip, watching them, their lips touching, the square to the circle, their legs identical, but their heads so different, standing hardly together, just touching. Just touching. Like hand in hand. Like lip to lip. Like body to body on a late night after work, the moon fractured out the window, a fall chill coming in, spiraling over Jack's lean hip to her full and moist skin. Joined, the two of them, different yet the same, each knowing the other, each knowing what the other didn't.

They were incredibly blessed, incredibly lucky, and incredibly happy. And they knew it. Their marriage was like that.

But the Fat Girl was alone. Doing things for Jack wouldn't bring him back. There was no more Jack. There was no more Jack. There was no more Jack.

The Fat Girl felt the shriek before she heard it, felt it rip from the bottom of her stomach, curl up her throat like a snake skinned with vomit, and spew out her mouth with a volume that made her put her hands over her own ears. Her body bent and flung itself, convulsion after tremor, and she shrieked and she howled and she wailed. She ripped her blouse, she tore at her hair, and the sound didn't stop even when she breathed in. Gasp and blow, gasp and blow, it was all loud, it was all raw, until finally, her voice guttered and choked into silence. But still the Fat Girl's mouth remained open, the snake still slithered out, climbed toward the ceiling, above which was her bedroom, their bedroom, the closet and Jack's shoes, the pillow and the shirt. The Fat Girl's silence was as dense as the shriek.

Eventually, she slumped to the floor, a new kind of exhaustion covering her. Stumbling even in a crawl, she made her way to the stepstools, their lips just touching. The Fat Girl pushed herself to her knees, lifted the broad and rounded circle, and placed it over the square. Intersecting them, sliding one unto the other, their legs blending, their tops different, but nesting. Falling to a sit, the Fat Girl lifted the stacked stools, placed them between her legs, rested her head on them, and spent the night.

Over the next few months, the Fat Girl made her way through routine. She went to work via the freeway. She did her job well, talking with her friends, helping her customers. She spent the evenings in her living room, and one night, she pulled the ottoman back where it belonged. She found a book Jack had been reading, on exercise and the elderly, and she placed it, open, on the table between their chairs. She watched the programs she enjoyed, she watched the programs he enjoyed, and the ones they both enjoyed together.

Once a week or so, she went to Sears on her lunch hour and she brought home a new item. The red retro ladder chair. Red placemats. A glorious vase which swirled with red and white and black, and she kept it filled with daffodils, the only spot of yellow in the room. A red and black and white suncatcher hung from the window. New red towels balanced on the rack. Bright red and furry rugs cushioned her feet when she stood at the stove or the sink.

Next to the table, a red and white bookshelf. On the top, she placed three framed photographs, gathered from a variety of walls and dressers around the house. Their wedding picture. A portrait for their twentieth anniversary. And a photo taken at Jack's company picnic, the two of them seated next to each other at a table, her plate brimmed with a burger and a hot dog, potato salad and cole slaw, and his loaded with fruits, veggies, and dip. They both had an ear of corn. Toasting each other, he held a bottle of water, she a wine cooler.

When everything was in place in the kitchen, almost six months after Jack's death, the Fat Girl finally climbed up on the stepstools. Both of them held her securely, as she finally felt sure they would. One by one, she lifted down the photo albums. There were a total of twelve.

Keeping them in order, the Fat Girl carried them across the black and white floor and she lined them up on the bookshelf, six to a row. Then, after fetching herself a cup of tea and some butter cookies, the Fat Girl sniffed the flowers in her vase, lit the red candles on either side, and then she selected the first of the albums. Centering it on a red placemat, she opened it.

"Oh, Jack," she said. "There you are."

The Fat Girl smiled, even as she reached for a tissue.

THE FAT GIRL IN DISGUISE

It wasn't easy being the Fat Girl in high school, not even during the summer. Everyone else was getting jobs, and the Fat Girl wanted one too. She was heading into her junior year and so she had to go to homecoming and prom or else the entire rest of high school would be totally bust. The Fat Girl needed to have some spending money, money for clothes and maybe a car. Especially clothes, because her mother said she wouldn't buy anything new until the Fat Girl did something about her weight.

The few friends the Fat Girl had were getting jobs at the mall, in the food court and in stores like Hot Topic and Aeropastale. But the Fat Girl just didn't feel comfortable in places like that. She didn't feel comfortable in any place, really, though she was okay hanging out with her friends, because they all were sort of different and so they didn't really fit in anywhere, except with each other. There was Jeannie with her buck teeth that her parents couldn't afford to fix. Amy with her skin condition. Taylor with her big stumpy shoe because she'd been born with one leg a full four inches shorter than the other. And the Fat Girl because of her size.

So the Fat Girl went to the mall, visited her friends during their breaks from their new jobs and tried to find a place where she could work too. She didn't want to stand out, she didn't want people to point at her and say, "What's someone like that doing working here?" The food court was completely impossible, because no matter where she worked, even if it had healthy food, people could point at her again and say, "Well, it's clear where you get your meals. Benefits here include free food?"

She thought she found the perfect spot when she saw the name. She thought she found the perfect spot when she saw the employees. The Large & Luscious Large Women's Clothing Boutique. Smallest size: 18. Largest size: None of your business!

The sign in the window, bold pink background, fat black curlicue print, actually said that. It made the Fat Girl smile. And the women who worked there, the women who rolled through the place, who ruled it with a wide sway of their hips and a thrust of their breasts, seemed so beautiful. They wore make-up and their clothes flowed and clung to their bodies like they were proud to be fat, like it was okay to be fat. Like they didn't want to hide. The Fat Girl had never seen large women move this way. The Fat Girl had never seen large women look up from the floor. So she squared her shoulders the way they did and she went in and sought out the store manager. "Are you hiring?" the Fat Girl asked.

The manager stared at her. The Fat Girl quickly crossed her arms over her stomach, bringing her shoulders back down to a slouch. "We are," the manager said.

"That's great," the Fat Girl said. "Could I have an application?"

"You? Well, sure you can, hon, but—" The manager glanced at a clerk rumbling by and the Fat Girl caught them both rolling their eyes. "You'd really want to work here? Why?"

"I just do. I think your clothes are great." Actually, the Fat Girl had never been inside this store before. But on her way to the counter, she'd passed jeans and tops that looked reassuringly like what all the girls were wearing. Just bigger. And longer. And no real waistline, though most of the shirts were what the Fat Girl thought were called A-line; the waistline was raised way up so it tucked in just beneath the breasts. And it was exactly those breasts of the shirts and blouses and dresses that the Fat Girl noticed the most. They were enormous. And often there was a dark outline in contrasting color curling around those parts, as if the clothes designers were attempting to spotlight large women's breasts. The Fat Girl glanced down at herself and doubted, even at her size, if she could ever hope to fill cups like that.

"I'm sorry, hon, I don't think it would work out," the manager said, picking up a magazine. "Have you tried Hot Topic? And I think Claire's is hiring." There were amazingly large women on the magazine's cover, who, even more amazingly, looked good. Looked wonderful. Looked like the women who worked at Large & Luscious. The Fat Girl wondered if she could look like that too.

As the magazine covered the manager's face, the Fat Girl knew she was being dismissed. Maybe she was too young? No one else seemed to be from high school here. Maybe the manager was afraid she wouldn't be able to offer enough hours? "I can work full time during the summer," the Fat Girl said. "And once school starts, I can work a couple evenings a week, maybe more, and full time on weekends. I'm a junior, and I'm way ahead on my graduation requirements, so I won't have much studying to do."

The manager lowered the magazine and sat for a moment, her eyes closed. The Fat Girl thought how she looked like a Buddha, about to impart wisdom. Or maybe acceptance. The Fat Girl hoped it was acceptance. "Sweetie, look," the manager said, eyes creasing open. "I think you should find someplace else. I just don't see how you could possibly think you'd fit in here. You know? You know, don't you?"

The Fat Girl jutted her chin out. It was always about fitting in, wasn't it, even here. Whether she was in English class or gym, joining the chess club or school choir, it was about fitting in. The Fat Girl wanted to fit in. She looked again behind her, at the racks and rows of clothes, size tabs proclaiming 18, 20, 22, 24. They went up to 28, and then the rest were grouped in a section called And More! The Fat Girl could see herself with these women, the women who worked at Large & Luscious. She could see herself sitting with them at lunch break, maybe sharing diet tips. She would laugh with them, maybe try on some of the clothes, learn how to dress so she still looked good, despite her size, like the models on that magazine. Imagine models of that size! The Fat Girl never knew there was such a thing! She could see herself sorting clothes, discovering the latest trends, helping shoppers choose, showing them to fitting rooms that were extra spacious and private. She could fit in. Especially here, she could! These women were just like her, only they'd figured out ways to be beautiful. The Fat Girl felt a wash of desperation. "Why?" she asked. "Why don't you think I'd fit?"

The girl running the cash register snorted. "You don't think it's obvious?" Her eyes seemed to narrow into laser beams, focusing right on the Fat Girl's stomach, which she'd hoped was camouflaged in her baggy jeans and smock top with spaghetti straps. But then, no one was wearing baggy jeans here. And they all had those A-line blouses, not smocks. The Fat Girl took a step backwards, then faced the manager again.

"I think I'd do okay," the Fat Girl said. "I'm real good at math, so I'd be fine at the cash register, and I love clothes." Actually, the Fat Girl hated clothes, or at least her clothes, or at least herself in her clothes, but she figured that would be the wrong thing to say. Her clothes just never seemed to do what they were supposed to. The Fat Girl read all the teen magazines and tried everything that was supposed to make her look better dressed than naked. But she looked awful either way. Though she'd never seen that magazine before, the one the manager held. The one with the beautiful large women. "I mean, if you're hiring, can't I apply? Isn't saying I can't, like, discrimination?"

The manager waited another minute, then pulled a sheet of paper off a pad. It turned out to be an application. "Take this home and fill it out," she said. "And really think about if you want to work here. I mean, really think about if this is the best place. And if you still think it is, then bring it back and we'll see. Make sure you show the application to your mother."

"Thank you!" The Fat Girl held the application tightly in both hands. "I'm sure I'll be back tomorrow!" Ecstatic, she left the store to meet Taylor on her lunch break.

At the food court, Taylor carefully wiped her hands before picking up the application. "What made you go in there?" she asked.

"I just thought it fit me," the Fat Girl said. She took a sip of her diet soda, loaded with ice, the way she liked it. "I mean, there was just something about being there. I mean… well, you know. You know me."

Taylor glanced over, then quickly away. "But isn't that place, like, for older ladies?"

The Fat Girl shrugged. "I thought so too, but you should see their clothes! They have the same kind of stuff other stores do, only bigger." She tapped the application. "I'm supposed to think about it, then bring this back tomorrow, but I'm going to go ahead and fill it out now." She dug through her purse for a pen. "I know they'll hire me." She stopped. "Oh…you know what? I wish I'd shopped there before I asked for the application. I bet they wouldn't turn me down if I showed up wearing their clothes. It would be, like, showing an interest, you know?"

Taylor's eyebrows went up, and the Fat Girl quickly bent over the application. Taylor said, "You'd wear clothes… from there?"

The Fat Girl sighed. "They've got the right sizes, Taylor. I think I'd fit." Her cheeks burned. She bet Taylor wouldn't like it if she looked at Taylor's leg and said, "You're going into Payless Shoe Source? You can wear shoes…from there?", her voice getting all squeaky and amazed too. Her group of friends usually didn't point out the others' deformities. The Fat Girl doggedly filled out the application.

After Taylor stumped back to work at Taco Bell, the Fat Girl carefully folded the application into her purse, and then wandered back over to Large & Luscious. She walked slowly by their windows a couple times, noticing that the manager was no longer behind the desk, and there was a different girl at the cash register. The Fat Girl went in and looked at the clothes. She shuffled through the 18s, but then decided to play it safe and go with the 20s. She didn't want to try them on; she didn't know if one of the girls she saw earlier was back in the dressing rooms, and she didn't want the manager to know that she came back to buy something. She wanted to make the manager think that she'd shopped here all along. After picking out a great pair of jeans with bright silver stitching on the back pockets, and an A-line top in a soft orange, a reddish brown pattern running contrast, she brought her selections to the cash register. She had some cash in her checking account; it would be enough to cover it.

"Would you like a gift receipt?" the girl behind the cash register asked.

"Oh, no, thanks," the Fat Girl said. "They're for me."

The cashier hesitated, then hit a button. "That's sixty-four eighty-one," she said. Her voice was cold.

The Fat Girl wondered why while she wrote out her check.

The next day, the Fat Girl dressed in her new clothes and stuffed cash for the bus into her pocket. She'd maybe have enough left over to buy a tall sugar-free fat-free latte at Starbucks with Jeannie and Amy, if they could arrange their breaks at the same time. Taylor had the day off, but she planned to meet the girls there too. "Mom!" the Fat Girl called. "I'm heading to the mall. I have to drop off an application."

Her mother looked up from the couch. Since she worked nights, her mom slept on the couch during the day, refusing to go to bed in a show of "being there" for her daughter, even if being there meant snoring in the living room instead of the bedroom. "You're dropping off an application dressed like that?" her mother asked.

The Fat Girl nodded. "These are clothes from the exact store where I'm applying. I thought it would be a good idea to show up in their stuff. Aren't these jeans cute?" The Fat Girl thought about twirling to show her mom the silver stitching, but instead, she stuck her hands in her pockets and thrust a hip out in a pose, kind of like the ones she saw on that magazine the day before.

"You bought those?"

"Yeah, I had enough money. It's like an investment, you know? I think it might help me get the job."

Her mother sat up and scrubbed her face. "Honey, why can't you ever buy clothes that fit? Those look awful."

The Fat Girl took a step backwards. "They're what's in fashion right now."

"But they don't fit! You're too—"

The Fat Girl ran out the door before her mother could finish. As she waited for the bus, she worked hard at shoving aside all the doubts that rose up now, rose up out of her mother's voice and thoughts and accusations. The Fat Girl would get this job. She would fit in at Large & Luscious. She would fit in some place for the very first time in her life and she would feel good and she'd smile and laugh and she'd have friends who knew exactly how she felt. Friends who would completely understand. Who could help her to be beautiful, despite this awful body, this awful, awful, ugly body. She would have friends who could teach her to look happy from the neck up, just like they looked happy from their necks up, while they all together, all of them, one huge mass of skin and sag and size, hated every inch that covered them. That covered the Fat Girl. They would understand the hatred that the Fat Girl sometimes felt was swallowing her whole.

When the Fat Girl walked through the revolving doors of the mall, she stopped for a moment, ducked into a corner. She straightened her new clothes, straightened her hair, straightened her shoulders. Pulling out the completed application from her purse, she smoothed it, snapped it smartly into shape, then headed for the escalator and Large & Luscious.

The manager was sorting clothes in a 50% off rack. The Fat Girl kept her head up and walked right to her.

"I'm back," the Fat Girl said. "And I've brought the application."

"I see." The manager took it, studied it, then looked back at the Fat Girl. "You bought those clothes here?"

"Yes, I did." The Fat Girl thought about striking the same pose she did with her mother, but decided against it. Instead, she stood tall, relaxed her hands at her sides, and continued looking the manager directly in the eye. In a self-confidence course with the guidance counselor at school, the counselor stressed the importance of maintaining eye contact.

"Okay. Come here a sec." The manager grabbed the Fat Girl's hand and led her over to a mirror. "Wait right here, hon."

The Fat Girl watched in the mirror as the manager went to the exact same racks the Fat Girl visited yesterday, and picked out the jeans and A-line top that the Fat Girl was wearing now. Calling to the girl at the cash register, the manager asked her to please put on these clothes and then come back out. The cashier glanced silently at the Fat Girl, then disappeared back by the dressing rooms. Returning, the manager carefully centered the Fat Girl in front of the mirror. Then, from a cunningly hidden slot, the manager extended a second mirror and snapped it next to the Fat Girl's reflection, doubling the size of the glass.

"For our larger customers," the manager explained. "Sometimes we need a bigger mirror. If we see someone come into the store like that, we slip out on the floor and pull out this addition, so the customer has a mirror at the ready, as if it's always here."

The Fat Girl nodded and looked at the empty glass next to her reflection. She wondered why she didn't spill over. Most days, she felt like she could fill five of those mirrors.

The cashier came back out, wearing the same clothes as the Fat Girl, and the manager waved her over. She centered the cashier in the mirror next to the Fat Girl.

"Okay," said the manager. "Look. Do you see the difference?"

The Fat Girl looked, earnestly looked, trying to see how the cashier might look better than she did. She wondered if she'd tied the top's sash in the wrong way, but both she and the cashier had it tied in the back, though the cashier's stayed firmly at the A-line, rather than drooping over her butt, like the Fat Girl's did. And, like yesterday, the cashier's breasts filled the blouse noticeably, straining the fabric, stretching the outline like boundaries on a map, with the forked river of her cleavage in the north. On the Fat Girl, it, well, gapped a bit. "In the… bosom," the Fat Girl said quietly, trying to pick the appropriate word. "In the…chest, we're different there."

The manager and the cashier caught each other's glances in the mirror. "Okay, go get changed," the manager said to the cashier. "Thanks for letting me put you on the spot. Wait—" she said when the cashier turned to go. "I've thought of something. Can you do me a favor and watch the store for a few minutes? Keep any customers busy out here. This won't take long." Then she grabbed the Fat Girl's hand again. "Come with me, hon."

They went into the back, and the manager picked out dressing room number seven. Opening the door, she waved the Fat Girl in, and then she came in too, after blocking the door open behind them. Just like on the floor, the manager centered the Fat Girl in front of the mirror. The Fat Girl noticed there was only one mirror in here, not on all three walls, like in other stores. In those other stores, when the Fat Girl tried things on, her body was splayed over the dressing room walls and she couldn't look away from herself, no matter how she tried. In Large & Luscious, she could control how much she saw, and when. She could look at herself when she chose to do so, when she was ready. The manager had the Fat Girl face the mirror like the Fat Girl was ready. But she felt her knees begin to shake.

"Okay." The manager stood behind the Fat Girl and placed her hands on her shoulders. Her touch was not heavy; rather, the Fat Girl felt momentarily soothed and her knees steadied out. "I probably shouldn't be doing this, but I really think it's important that you see. Show me the waistline of the jeans."

The Fat Girl looked at the manager's eyes through the reflection in the mirror. The manager didn't blink. She didn't look down. The Fat Girl also didn't look down, but she reached for the A-line's hem and raised it to just above her waist. The manager nodded.

"Now take off the belt."

The Fat Girl didn't move.

Carefully, the manager reached around. She found the belt's buckle and undid it. And then unwound it the two times it was wrapped around the Fat Girl's middle. She unwound it through layers of denim scrunched together, folded in like the top of a drawstring sack. And she pulled the belt free.

The Fat Girl's brand new jeans fell straight down, like a stage curtain revealing in reverse, hitting the floor with the softest of shushes.

The manager and the Fat Girl both stood in silence, looking into the mirror. Into the reflection, and into what was in front of them both. The hugeness of the Fat Girl's hips, as smooth and flat as skipping stones. Her gigantic thighs, her massive calves, trailing like willow branches toward a puddle of socks whose tight ribbing couldn't cling. Looking and looking at the blue veins, standing out sharply against the white of the Fat Girl's skin, trickling like a river about to go dry. The Fat Girl drew in a breath, and against her stomach, the A-line went flat, then hung limply.

The manager said, barely above a whisper, "Now do you see? Do you see, hon?"

The Fat Girl looked, swallowed, and reached for her jeans and belt. "No," she said at the same volume. "I belong here. I do. I fit in. I thought you'd understand."

The manager turned away. "I'm sorry," she said. "I'm sorry, but no. Please…go talk to your mother. Please get some help." She left the dressing room and gently closed the door.

The Fat Girl fastened her jeans, raising the curtain and realigning her reflection with her reality. Then she ran out of Large & Luscious. She fought the tears that tried to well, but couldn't gain purchase in dried sockets, fought the sobs that pulled at her ribcage, that made her skin stretch painfully beneath the clothes that could fold over her once, twice, three times. She didn't go talk to her friends. She didn't go talk to her mother. She didn't fit in anywhere and her isolation fell over her face, filled her mouth, and glutted her body to bursting.

Stuffing her hands in her pockets, holding up the jeans that threatened to fall despite the double-wrapped belt, the Fat Girl left the mall. But she had nowhere to go.

THE FAT GIRL'S SACRIFICE

The Fat Girl began noticing the glances around the same time she noticed her ribcage. The looks were mostly from people she knew, or people who had at least seen her before with some regularity, even if they didn't know who she was. The Fat Girl worked in a mall, at the Large & Luscious Large Women's Clothing Boutique, and there were many people she recognized every day that she didn't know by name. These were the people that clerked at other stores or ran the restaurants in the food court or didn't work in the mall at all, but who walked around and around in the hour before the mall officially opened. They usually stared at her, then looked away. But then, the Fat Girl noticed them noticing her differently. Not looking away so fast. And some, she caught looking over their shoulders at her as she looked over her shoulder at them.

Why?

She was used to those quick stares, the intakes of breath, the eyebrows shooting up, then lowering in accusation. How could you let yourself get like that, she imagined them saying, though they never actually did, not out loud. Some people snorted, though they might have been clearing their throats. Some people laughed, though maybe they'd thought of something funny.

The Fat Girl didn't think there was anything funny about her. Certainly not her breasts, large unkneaded bread loaves that she picked up each morning and dropped into bra cups before hoisting them off her tummy with the shoulder straps. Straps that dug, no matter how large the bra, no matter how she extended the clips. Not her stomach, grown now into two, the first curving into a crease at her navel, the next falling down in front of her thighs. She still thought of them as tummies, the word she'd used since childhood, though she did pluralize it and sometimes referred to them as Siamese twins. Every day, she tucked the twins into size 6X underwear and hoped that by pulling the briefs up to where her waist should be, the crease between tummies wouldn't be visible from the outside. And her thighs certainly weren't funny either, rashed and rubbed raw as they were.

So the Fat Girl told herself the giggles couldn't possibly be for her.

But now the regulars weren't laughing. They weren't even snorting. They were holding their gaze, then checking her out again once she passed by.

One night at home, after finishing supper, after finishing dessert, half of which she left on her plate and glanced at from time to time in surprise, the Fat Girl lay on her couch and scratched an itch under her right breast. American Idol was on, and she hummed along with the songs and thought about how much better she could do, if only she could bear to go on stage. The Fat Girl had a wonderful voice, deep and earthy, evenly mixed with silk and gravel. By the age of three, she'd been plunked in sequins and set on a stage, and she clearly remembered singing, "Help Me Make It Through The Night," complete with tears running down her chubby cheeks, to a State Fair audience when she was four. By the time the tween years hit, she went from chubby to fat, and her mother said she went from cute to horrific, from VW Bug to Hindenburg, and the only singing the Fat Girl did was in the high school chorus. At concerts, they stuck her in the middle of the back row, and she never had any solos. Not even a duet. Once, though, when the school did a musical and the lead was a girl that couldn't sing, but boy, could she act and flit about the stage with point-the-way breasts and easy-flowing hips, the Fat Girl stood behind the curtain with a microphone and thrust her voice into the thin girl's hollow lungs, her flapping silent lips. The Fat Girl was given credit in the program. But when she came out to bow with the cast, she was once again in the back row.

So the Fat Girl was humming along with American Idol when she scratched and felt a bump. Right under her breast, it was, and it was hard. At first, she panicked, but then she found one under her other breast as well. Scooting further down the couch, sliding her head from the armrest until it was flat on the cushion, the Fat Girl lifted her shirt and stretched out as best she could, running her hands up her sides and then under the moist folds of her breasts. And she realized she was feeling the top of her ribcage.

What was that doing there? She hadn't been dieting, at least not in an organized way, though she hadn't been as hungry of late. The Fat Girl drummed her fingers along her bones, and she tried to remember the last time she'd identified them. She couldn't. Yet there the bones were, a part of her skeleton, a part of what held her together, carried her around, and they were firm and solid. She could follow them until they disappeared on either side of her, dipping into soft and round back flab.

Excited now, the Fat Girl stood up and stripped, shimmering her hands down her body, over her stomach, her hips, down her thighs, as far as she could reach. And it seemed to her that there was just a bit more of a point to her hipbones; she had to press, but they were there. And her thighs, if she stood in her normal wide-kneed stance, were not touching all the way down. There were gaps, peekaboo holes, and the Fat Girl put her hands at her waist and wondered.

She hadn't been eating as much because she wasn't as hungry…and the Fat Girl was amazed at the gift. Usually, her appetite tore at her from the inside out, spreading in spasms from the pit of her gut, fanning out like a cataclysm of need. She ate as she laughed and she ate as she cried, and she ate until she finally felt satisfied. No longer empty. Deep inside herself, she could roll with her life, take the next step and the next, until it was time to eat again.

Standing there, on the stage of her living room floor, the music from American Idol playing around her, there was no one in front of the Fat Girl to block her from view. There was no hunger and no eating. The hurricane within her unspiraled and fell silent. The Fat Girl wanted to weep.

The hunger went silent for weeks, and then into months, and the Fat Girl discovered more bones. Every night, when she went to bed, she explored her fingers over herself and made discoveries. More and more ribs. Pelvic hills. Hip bones, collar bone, wrists and shoulders and elbows. Her skin hung like a flag in mid-August, and she began to walk in the morning, joining the lappers around the mall, taking in two rounds, then three and four and more, and arriving for work just in time. The exercise helped, but her skin was still flappy, and so she began to wear long sleeves and slacks.

And the people. How the Fat Girl was noticed! Clerks nodded at her as she walked on her lunch break, and they smiled at her every morning. The walkers waved at her and she waved back, and some even began calling out as she chugged by. "Lookin' good!" "Great work!" "You're my inspiration!"

The Fat Girl had never been an inspiration before.

At work, the Large & Luscious employees weren't quite sure what to do. They fluttered around her and admired and complimented, but the Fat Girl could see past their words. They wanted to know what she was doing. What diet are you following, they asked and she honestly answered, not a one. What pill are you taking, they asked, and she shook her head. Well, how are you doing it, they said, exasperated, you're clearly doing something, you're melting away! You look the best we've ever seen you! The Fat Girl shrugged and smiled and said she only stopped eating, because she really wasn't hungry much anymore. And they gasped at the audacity. Is everything okay? the manager asked, Are you sure you're all right? And the Fat Girl laughed and twirled and showed off how wonderful she looked; of course she was all right! She wondered if she would be fired if she got too skinny.

The Fat Girl watched her clothing size drop like a February temperature, from 32 to 28, 28 to 24, all the way down to 18. At 18, she could buy clothes in the misses section, and she felt like a miss, a young girl of discovery and innocence. Large & Luscious didn't have a misses section, their clothing sizes started at 18. The Fat Girl still shopped there too, but she began exploring the other stores, checking out their selections. She had a real waist, a solid indentation between her breasts and her hips. She loved the way her body curved in like the swells of an ocean, the movement at once feminine and fluid. She bought her first belt in years.

Then there was the day a man who worked in the shoe store asked her out on a date; the Fat Girl felt positively nauseous with shock. She'd been feeling a bit queasy of late, she'd noticed, and quickly attributed it to her body's trying to catch up with her loss, but when the man asked her out, she ran into the nearest ladies' room and threw up. Good, she thought, there's two more pounds, and I'll be a 16 before you know it.

She let the shoe salesman touch her on the second date, and once he started to touch her, he wouldn't stop. Not that she wanted him to; she was uncharted territory, and she felt her body flow up to his fingers, his lips, and his center as if she'd been waiting her whole life just for this. It was amazing, it was, and she got caught up in the surge, and her body liquefied into the sea. No, not the sea, not anymore, not even a lake, but a pond. A salty pond, a beautiful, clear, warm little pond, and she was soaked through and elated.

She began to date him every night.

Yet through it all, through the no eating and the walking, the love-making and the shopping, the long minutes spent in front of her newly purchased full-length mirror, the Fat Girl waited for energy. With each pound lost, she braced herself for an uprising, a tirelessness that would lightning-flash through her muscles, her newly acquired muscles, and would make her want to shimmy and dance. But it didn't come. As the Fat Girl walked around and around the mall, the tiredness sucked at her ankles, and when she worked, it grabbed onto her knees and her elbows. During love-making, there were times when she let herself just lay there, sinking into the mattress as her lover worked hard above, until he touched her shoulder or her hip like a jockey with a whip and she moved into rhythm again. The Fat Girl noticed the tiredness and the queasiness, and she told herself it was just her body dropping its addictions. Addictions to sugar, to fat, to warm butter and melted cheese and chocolate so dark, it was black. Breaking addictions leads to exhaustion, she told herself, this was only her body trying to acclimate. Her body, lost for a lifetime in barriers of fat, of secrets and desires and sadness and solitude, just didn't know how to be normal. It would take some time to adjust to this switch from being large and invisible to small and spotlighted. How was a body to make sense of that? The Fat Girl grew dizzy just thinking about it.

It was late at night after her lover's departure, when the Fat Girl was lying in bed, that she found another lump. A real lump. She was still new to the luxury of a love-soaked warm bed and as soon as she heard her door close, she stretched, arms high overhead, then ran her fingers down her entire body and dazzled herself at how much less entire could be. But on the second trip, her finger lurched over a hard spot in her smaller right breast, now more like a hamburger bun than a bread loaf. She told herself she didn't feel it, but then she tried again, and found the lump without hunting. It was the size of a marble, a shooter, like the glass ones she used to play with when she was a child. It was hard like a bone, but its own little island, and far away from the surface of her skeleton. She rubbed it, over and over, and there was no sleep that night.

The next day, her doctor raved over her weight loss, over the health benefits, the longevity, the self-esteem. He hadn't seen her in a year, since he treated her for a vile sinus infection, and she was, he said, half the patient she was then. But when the Fat Girl spoke of her lump, and when he himself felt it, the doctor dropped into silence.

Mammogram, ultrasound, biopsy, and hospital. For a moment, as she lay on the gurney and waited to be wheeled into surgery, the Fat Girl wished for her hurricane back. She wished that the cessation of hunger had never occurred, and with it, the arrival of this new body and its hidden sewage.

But she wished that only for a moment. The nurse who held her hand as they wheeled her away told her how beautiful she looked, fitting so slim on the gurney, nothing hanging over, the sheets draping her naked body like a ball gown. The Fat Girl reached for her ribcage and glowed.

She left the hospital one breast lighter, but newly heavy with the darkest of news. She was told of spreading and metastisizing, of sticking and lingering, of cocktails and chemo and rayguns.

The clothing temperature dipped further, from 16 to 12, 12 to 8, 8 to 4. Wherever she went, the Fat Girl received pinches and offers and pats, and after arming herself quickly with a prosthesis, she still glowed. She was beautiful, and she knew it. Everyone could see it, they could see her, and she knew it. It took illness, but she was here, and they saw her. She was on stage. She was in the spotlight. It was worth it.

Still, the job disappeared first, and it took with it the mall, the walkers and the clerks and the smiles. And then the shoe salesman left too. There wasn't much time, but there were a few other men, and as soon as they saw the Fat Girl naked, one breast missing, the other slacking, they drained their drinks and left.

In hospice, the nurses brushed what was left of the Fat Girl's hair, and they called her lovely. It still made her smile. Alone in her room, the sides up on her bed, the Fat Girl tried to stretch and run her hands down the xylophone length of her body. She took the nurses' compliments, how beautiful you are!, and drew them up to her chin, warming herself as she withered away. A 4 to a 2 to a 0. What else was there after zero? Nothing.

The Fat Girl hugged her skeleton. Around her, she heard she was beautiful. The word floated in pink and cream and lavender, as lacy as filigree, and soft. The Fat Girl was beautiful.

It was worth the sacrifice. Lowering her long-lashed eyelids against her alabaster and pronounced cheekbones, the Fat Girl breathed out.

THE FAT GIRL'S GLORIOUS BUTTERBALL

The Fat Girl didn't know she was pregnant until the butterball baby squirted from between her thighs and into the ER doctor's surprised hands. The Fat Girl still didn't believe it as she heard that alien cry, a voice rusty with no use at all, but when the butterball baby settled against the Fat Girl's breasts, she believed. She swelled with belief. Her mouth dropped open with belief. And her eyes overflowed with it.

"You didn't know you were pregnant?" the doctor asked. Everyone, the nurses, the doctor, even the Fat Girl herself, seemed to be holding incredibly still, as if one wrong move would shatter the scene and render it into hallucination.

The Fat Girl shook her head. She'd thought she had appendicitis. She kept having cramps throughout her workday at the Large & Luscious Large Women's Clothing Boutique in the mall, and when she finally doubled over by the cash register, the manager insisted she go to the hospital. The Fat Girl's husband, alerted by a cell phone call, was on his way to the ER right now, expecting to find his wife being trundled off to emergency surgery, and instead, he would find a family.

"You didn't notice your periods went missing? You didn't feel the baby move?" a nurse asked.

The Fat Girl shook her head again, looking down at this unexpected baby, quiet now, having somehow managed to find the nipple on one of the Fat Girl's incredible basketball breasts. "I don't have my period very often," the Fat Girl said, "because of my size, I guess. And I've been feeling things, but I thought it was…you know…like gas maybe."

"This baby's been well-hidden," the doctor said. "Buried, you might say."

The butterball was a little girl, an amazingly healthy little girl, everything intact, and a beautiful pink color. The Fat Girl watched as the cord was cut, separating her from the daughter she never knew she was connected to, and even though everything was so new, the Fat Girl felt a sense of loss. She wanted to stuff the baby back inside, coil the cord like a hose reel, return the baby to the womb the Fat Girl didn't know she had. She wanted to experience everything again, but with understanding this time. With knowledge. Those strange fishy feelings that swarmed her large belly, that made her laugh and squeeze her cheeks together, expecting an outburst of flatulence. Now she wanted to feel the flutter of fish again and know that they were from a baby. This baby. Her baby. The brush of fingers, the muted kick from a foot, a slow roll of an entire graceful body. The Fat Girl wanted to recognize being a Russian nesting doll, harboring a smaller version of herself deep inside. But the pregnancy was officially over, and the Fat Girl and the butterball two complete individuals now.

A nurse took the baby, diapered her, and wrapped her in a blanket. Another nurse called up to maternity and explained that they would have two new surprise residents.

The Fat Girl heard her husband's voice, calling her name. "Babe, I'm in here," she called, and she wondered if she would have to change her usual endearment for him, now that there really was a babe in the family. She held the butterball again, cradled in one arm, pillowed on a breast, and when her husband parted the curtain and took in the scene, the Fat Girl nearly laughed at the size of his eyes, suddenly exploding in his heavy face.

"Oh my god," he said.

"Babe," she said, "I guess I was pregnant. We have a baby girl."

He moved alongside the bed and looked. The baby was asleep now, and when he reached out and stroked her face, she rosebudded her lips and the Fat Girl felt herself just melt. Flat away. Her blood gone warm and her breasts soft and her vision newly sharpened and protective.

She caught the doctor and the nurses sneaking looks at them, the three of them, yes, but especially her husband and herself, and she knew what they were wondering. How did they do it? How did they conceive? With those two bellies, how could they…reach? Connect? The Fat Girl turned away from them and instead looked into the deepest brown eyes in the world, which happened to belong to her husband. "Oh, babe," she whispered. "Look what we've done."

When the Fat Girl returned home forty-eight hours later, she found herself in a surprise fairyland. At the top of the stairs, to the right, the guest room had been transformed into a nursery. "When I told the girls at Large & Luscious," her husband said, "they went crazy. They came here and helped me with this."

The room was now a gentle soft pink, nearly matching the little girl's newborn complexion. The ragtag spare furniture, leftover from dorm rooms and a newlywed apartment, was removed, and in its place was a crib, a changing table, a dresser and a rocker, all in white. There were puffy stuffed plush things everywhere, on the walls, on the floor, on a set of shelves, in the crib. Bears, hearts, unicorns, angels. The pink and white reminded the Fat Girl of cotton candy, wispy, sweet, blow-away on a hot day, and light as air. She noticed with gratitude that the rocking chair was extra wide and deep and also very sturdy.

"Look, Butterball," she said to the baby. "We didn't even know you were on the way, but now it's like you've always been here. You've been welcomed home." She sat in the rocker, found the ancient rhythm of maternity, and looked around. Supplies were stocked and ready to go. Diapers, wet wipes, t-shirts, sleepers. Things that had never been in this house before. She smiled at her husband. "Everything is different now, isn't it."

He nodded. "It's amazing. We sure weren't planning for this." Slowly, he lowered himself like a grand circus elephant onto one knee, then the other. He wrapped an arm around her and joined her in her rock, looking into the baby's sleeping face.

"Well, it's not like we prevented it either. We just thought we couldn't conceive. Because, well…you know." She poked his cheek.

He poked her back, then kissed her. "Are you tired? Do you need anything?"

"Actually, I am tired. I kept her in the hospital room with me last night. Rooming in, they call it. She was up quite a bit. Probably why she's sleeping now. Do you want to hold her for a while and I'll go take a nap? You can always put her in the crib, if there's something else you have to do." The Fat Girl noticed what looked like a white and pink transistor radio on the dresser. "We even have a baby monitor! We'll hear her as soon as she makes a peep."

"Sure." Her husband's large hands swept softly between the baby's bottom and the Fat Girl's arm, and the Fat Girl noticed how tiny the baby seemed, tucked into the crook of his elbow. This still gave him one hand free to lift himself from the floor, and then help her to her feet. Carefully, in a move as gentle as the spreading of a quilt, he sank into the white rocker. The baby didn't stir. The Fat Girl knew her husband wouldn't leave the chair, wouldn't put the baby in the crib, unless he absolutely had to.

"The nurses showed me how to express my milk. I brought home a couple bottles. They're in the insulated bag if you need to feed her before I wake up." She pointed toward one of the free gifts from the hospital.

He nodded, though the Fat Girl wasn't sure how much he really heard. He was already lost in his movement, in the sight of his baby.

The Fat Girl kissed them both on the tops of their heads, wincing as she felt her bending produce a gush of blood from between her legs. She hadn't had a period in so long that she'd forgotten what this felt like, and after childbirth, the blood was so much more profuse and powerful. She used their bathroom to clean up, to change into another one of the large after-birth maternity pads, and then took off her shoes and lowered herself, carefully, gently, onto her bed. She had a new respect for her body these days. She closed her eyes, listening to the quiet of the house, and waited to hear that quiet tossed aside for the first time by a baby's cry.

As she tried to rest, as she tried to stay awake and listen, she thought of the phone call she placed to her mother from the hospital. Her mother had at first been dumbfounded.

"You didn't even tell me you were pregnant!" she'd said.

"Mom, I told you. I didn't know." The Fat Girl had glanced over at the clear plastic bassinet where her daughter slept peacefully. The Fat Girl was still amazed.

"How could you not know? I mean, even you, even at your size, couldn't you tell…" Her mother lapsed into silence for one brief minute, then continued on. "Well, I'm happy for you. For both of you. I am. I'll make some arrangements and stay with you for a while, help you out. Come see this surprise package."

"Oh, no, Mom, that's not necessary—"

"Yes, it is." Whenever the Fat Girl heard her mother's voice over the phone, she involuntarily pictured tiny scissors slithering into her eardrum. "You probably don't know the first thing about a child. You didn't even know she was coming. Things are going to have to change now, you know."

"Change?" The Fat Girl looked again at the baby sleeping no more than three feet away. Things had already monumentally changed.

"You both have to lose weight now. It's no longer an option. You can't risk your health anymore. What if you both die of heart attacks before that child is five years old? Who is going to raise her? Me? Not a chance. I don't want to go through all of that again."

The Fat Girl shifted in her hospital bed and listened to it creak. Even when they rolled her down the hall to her room from the ER, they hadn't put the sides up. They wouldn't fit around her.

"And you need to teach your child good habits. She can't learn them from you, the way you are now. For God's sake, by the time she's walking, you guys will be guests on Maury Povich. He's always doing shows on gigantic babies. Poor things."

Back at home now, her eyes closed, listening to the silence, imagining her husband in the guest room, the baby's fairyland, rocking, rocking, the butterball swaddled with her tiny hands folded next to her mouth, the Fat Girl wondered why she hadn't asked her mother how it was that this teeny tiny woman who never weighed over a hundred and two, who treated eating like a science and not a pleasure, managed to produce the Fat Girl.

But even so. The baby was so tiny. So tiny that the Fat Girl's body had engulfed her, hidden her, not even letting the Fat Girl's brain know that there was a life growing inside of her. Not even letting her heart know. Maybe this new respect, respect for a body that could grow and produce a child with no exterior effort, wasn't earned. Maybe it was a body that swallowed a child until disgorgement just couldn't be stopped. Until the doctor's trained hands reached inside and yanked the child out of harm's way. And then he replaced her into the most dangerous arms of all. Right back in the path of harm.

The Fat Girl ran her hands over her large body, the body she knew every inch of and hated, the body her husband knew every inch of and loved, and she worried.

Several days later, the Fat Girl was in the baby's room, without the baby. Her breasts ached. She hadn't nursed for several hours, instead expressing milk into a bottle and handing it over to her mother, who claimed that the Fat Girl would probably feed the little girl too much. "You won't know when to stop," her mother said in her scissors voice. "You never know when to stop."

The Fat Girl could hear the baby downstairs, crying, a mewl which seemed to tighten around the Fat Girl's neck like a garrote. Her mother's voice was there too, talking to the baby, talking, talking, and the Fat Girl didn't need to hear the words to know what her mother was saying. She'd known that tone all of her life, though it had sharpened considerably the first time she came home after starting college, with the freshman fifteen settled firmly on her hips.

College was the first time that the Fat Girl felt freedom, and it was the first time that she realized she hadn't been free all along. At home, her mother cared for her, providing her with three meals every day, served for her on her plate, like clockwork. Breakfast, a bowl of cereal and a glass of skim milk. Lunch, a half-sandwich with one piece of bologna, no condiments, three carrot sticks or three celery sticks, and a sliced apple. Sometimes a pear. Supper, a small piece of meat and a ladleful of canned vegetables. Saturdays meant one scoop of ice cream for dessert. Snacks were twice a day, at three o'clock and at nine o'clock, and they were always two packaged cookies and more skim milk. In between meals, the Fat Girl could have water.

At college, the Fat Girl discovered food. She discovered fast food hamburgers and she discovered brownies. Soda.

Chips and dip. She still firmly remembered the day she walked into an ice cream shop and realized that there was more to ice cream than chocolate, vanilla, strawberry, and neapolitan. It was almost frightening at first, all the choices, all the flavors, all the textures and treatments of food. But then…it was a joy.

Now, the Fat Girl rocked by herself in her baby's room. Already, her mother had the butterball on a schedule. If the baby cried and it wasn't time for a bottle, she just kept crying. If she finished a little bottle and was still hungry, she cried some more. Every time the Fat Girl thought about intervening, she stopped, looked at herself, and then her mother. Tiny, more than petite, wearing a size zero after it was shrunk in the dryer. Sometimes, her mother shopped in the girls' departments. Not juniors. Girls. The Fat Girl only shopped at Large & Luscious.

When the mewling stopped, the Fat Girl fell asleep in the rocker and that's where her husband found her when he came home. "What are you doing up here?" he asked. "The baby is downstairs. She's crying."

"I know. My mother has her. I was just so tired." The Fat Girl heaved herself up and felt the now familiar rush of blood.

Her husband steadied her. "Your mother is cooking supper again. I already saw the plates. A skinless chicken breast. A scoop of vegetables." He hugged her. "That can't be enough. Not for you. Not for someone who just gave birth, who is bleeding, who is supposed to be feeding her baby."

The Fat Girl shrugged. "My mother says it is. She should know. Just look at her. She's had babies. She had me."

They went downstairs and the Fat Girl sat at her place. She looked at her plate. Colorless chicken. Canned green beans. On the couch, surrounded by pillows, the baby cried. The Fat Girl's husband went to pick her up.

"Leave her," the Fat Girl's mother said. She held up the empty little bottle. "I just fed her. She's fine. She just doesn't know how to feel full yet."

The Fat Girl's husband kissed the baby's cheek. He brought her to the Fat Girl, put her in the Fat Girl's arms. The butterball nuzzled and the Fat Girl's breasts ached and felt like they were reaching. Stretching beyond the confines of the Fat Girl's clothes, to surround the butterball. To fill her. The Fat Girl felt the ache spread, soar through the rest of her body. The sounds of the baby's cry, still soft, still plaintive, hit the Fat Girl's body like splats of warm rain, gentle now, but threatening to become a full-fledged storm.

"She's fine," the Fat Girl's mother said.

"I'll take her for a bit," the Fat Girl said. "You need a break, Mom. I'll eat in a while. I can wait." Carefully, humming softly, the Fat Girl returned to the nursery and settled into the rocker. Balancing the baby against her shoulder, kissing the pink cheek, the Fat Girl unbuttoned her shirt. Then she rested the baby, wiggling, on her lap, while she stripped off the shirt and removed her bra. Rocking, humming, looking down at the undulations of her own body, the Fat Girl put the baby to one breast and felt the little lips latch on. The letting down of her milk felt like an internal waterfall and the Fat Girl felt the warmth flow from her to her daughter. The baby sank into a stomach roll, safe like a cradle, and was blanketed by one breast while being nourished by the other. The baby fit into the Fat Girl like an extra little roll of fat, a beautiful, glorious little roll of fat. The Fat Girl's body puddled around her, molded around her, and protected her just as it had for nine months. Tucked away deep inside, there was no safer place. And now, the Fat Girl curled around her baby again and she felt the padded wall her body provided, between the baby and the world.

The baby sucked and sucked, and the Fat Girl felt the relief and joy of it. The baby's limbs relaxed, quieted, and when she was placed on the second breast, her mouth kept going, but she fell asleep.

"What are you doing?" The Fat Girl's mother flew into the room, all angles and sharp edges. "She's had her bottle, it's not time to eat! Not for another four hours!" She surged toward the baby, her fingers out like pitchforks. "Get your clothes on! Look at you!"

"Look at you!" the Fat Girl's husband echoed. "Oh," he said softly. "Just look at you."

The Fat Girl pulled the butterball further into her body. The baby sighed, slipped off the nipple, and sucked in her lower lip, a bead of white dripping down her chin. It was a kewpie smile. "Mom," the Fat Girl said, quietly so as not to wake the baby, but firmly enough so her mother could hear and believe. "Mom, go home."

In bed, in the middle of the night, after the interruption and peace of a three o'clock feeding, the Fat Girl and her husband each lay on their sides, the butterball baby between them. Downstairs, the sleeper sofa in the family room, the new makeshift guest room, was folded in.

The Fat Girl looked at the baby, asleep in the valley between her two mountainous parents. They rose over her, protective, strong, immovable. The Fat Girl's form was more curved than her husband's, her body still female and soft in its weight. Her husband, solid, was a fortress. Sleeping surrounded by safety, the baby flew open her hands and settled them above her head.

Her husband yawned. "We should really put her back in her crib," he said. "We should both get sleep while we can. She sure is a hungry little thing."

The Fat Girl nodded. By the time she lumbered out of bed and scooped the baby up, her husband's eyes were already closed. His snores rolled down the hallway before she reached the nursery, and she smiled at the sound.

Carefully, she lowered the butterball into her crib. The baby instantly resumed her hands-over-her-head posture. Already, the Fat Girl knew that this was the baby's deep sleep pose. Nothing would wake her now but hunger. And already, the Fat Girl knew the differences in the cries, what meant hunger, what meant tired, what meant discomfort, what meant simply I don't know what else to do but cry. The Fat Girl knew that one especially well, and it was the one that hurt her the most, and made her cradle the baby and fiercely rock it all away.

Now, she looked at her daughter and pulled the quilt up to her chest. The nightlight cast a moony glow and the night drew like a blanket around the room. The blackness wasn't alarming, but only quiet, and the Fat Girl settled into the rocker. From down the hall, her husband snored, and in the nursery, the rocker had already developed a familiar rhythmic creak.

The Fat Girl closed her eyes and listened to it all, and waited for the sound, still a surprise, that would hurtle her to her feet, into the next moment, and then the next, and into a solid passage of days and nights and the growth of this child. The cry of the glorious baby.

THE FAT GIRL GOES STEADY

When the Fat Girl turned forty-eight, she began seeing Death on every corner. She knew that most people saw Death on her corner for years, that everyone assumed she would someday drop dead of a heart attack because she hadn't taken good care of herself. What else could account for the undulating roll upon roll upon roll, gravity pulling down, skin falling in waves from her abdomen to her thighs, from her thighs to her knees, from her knees to her calves, and finally her ankles cresting over her shoes? People never thought about all the trys and all the failures, the diets, the pills, the exercise routines, which always knocked off a few pounds and then stalled out. It could be glands, the Fat Girl supposed, though the doctor said no. It could be genes. But no matter what it was, no matter what she ate, the Fat Girl was still the Fat Girl. And if that was to be the case, then why not eat good, if eating well and eating good were going to bring about the same results anyway?

But at forty-eight, the Fat Girl felt a shift. A co-worker died of breast cancer. The Fat Girl had worked with her at the Large & Luscious Large Women's Clothing Boutique in the mall for over twenty years; they'd started the same day.

Daily life in a mall was like living in a small town. Inside the store was the Fat Girl's family, and outside the store were the other families and they all knew each other in the vaguest sort of way, like neighbors across the street or down the block. Whenever there was a crisis at any store or any kiosk, everyone knew about it. When the Fat Girl was a new employee, and even after she'd worked there for ten years, all the tragedies seemed to happen to the older folks. But now, they didn't seem so old. There was the Large & Luscious cancerous co-worker. A guy in a shoe store had a stroke. A woman at Sears turned up with ALS. Shoe store man was fifty-two, Sears lady, fifty-five, co-worker, forty-nine. And that was maybe the most disturbing thing of all...it wasn't like Large & Luscious was Heart Attack Central even with all the Fat Girls; there'd only been the breast cancer. The women of Large & Luscious ranged in size from 18 to off the charts, but fat didn't seem to be the death factor at the mall. Death happened to everyone, whether or not they were fat, whether they worked in the food court or in a sports store. The issue was age. And now the Fat Girl was forty-eight.

Forty-eight and The Fat Girl. And while fat didn't necessarily seem like a factor, it still didn't seem like a good combination with age. The Fat Girl tried to console herself with images of her manager, and the other Large & Luscious Women who were even larger than the Fat Girl. If her manager, who far outweighed the Fat Girl, could still be kicking at sixty-three, why wouldn't the Fat Girl?

But still. Death loomed.

So the Fat Girl tried. Again. She ate fruit for breakfast and salads at lunch (though supper was still up for grabs). She showed up to work early to walk one laborious lap around the second floor of the mall, her thighs swishing, her joints aching, her lungs turning inside out by the time she dragged herself across the threshold of the store. She took low-dose aspirin and researched vitamins. But she just couldn't shake the thought of the inevitability of her death.

It had never been so close before. Death always seemed like a shadowed feather bed, a place she would want to go to rest someday, to close her eyes and sleep a sleep that left her fully free. A place she would want to go, at the end of a very, very, very long life.

But right now, it was a place she didn't want to go at all. And the Fat Girl didn't want to start down any of Death's curvy paths either. The things that happened to bodies as they grew older, the things that were done to them! Strange lumps. Chemo. Age spots. Wrinkles and amputations. Drugs, drugs, and more drugs. Support hose and braces, walkers and wheelchairs. The Fat Girl didn't want to do what she would desperately do in order to stay alive, and she didn't want to die either. It was as simple as that.

Then one day, as the Fat Girl lumbered around her lap of the mall, she saw Death sitting at a table in Starbucks. He had a latte and one of their great cheese danish, which she hadn't had in weeks. There was no scythe in sight, but the trademark hooded long black coat covered Death's face and rivered to the floor, making him stand out among the other pastel and white summer-clad caffeine junkies. Making him stand out anywhere. The Fat Girl crossed to the other side of the aisle, even though it meant going against traffic. She wanted as much space between her and Death as possible. As she passed, the hood moved, just a bit, in her direction. Death reached for his danish. He brandished it. The Fat Girl moved quickly away, arriving at Large & Luscious out of breath.

Over the next several weeks, Death appeared at the bus stop at the mall entry, then at the Happy Belly Deli across from the Fat Girl's apartment, and at the produce section of her grocery store, right by the spinach. Every morning, he sat at Starbucks. Each time, the hood insinuated in her direction, and each time, the Fat Girl walked away in what was, for her, a trot. She never saw his face. His hands were covered by his sleeves.

One night, before bed, the Fat Girl stood in front of the full-length mirror she'd bought, thinking that if she looked at herself naked every night, it would motivate her to lose weight. It hadn't, but it provided marvelous motivation for self-deprecation and hatred instead. The Fat Girl stood there and stared. She only had the light on in the hallway, so the air was gray, and she'd hoped to soften her own impact. But nothing would soften it. Her breasts hung so low, the nipples seemed like forgotten thumbtacks about to disappear into flabby balloons. Her navel was forever lost in a crease. Her joints were all covered by hanging dimpled flesh, and the Fat Girl wondered for a moment what the sharp poke of an elbow would feel like, the fluid bend of a knee. The only way she could see her pubic area was to scoop up her stomach in both forearms and lift, and then she could just barely glimpse the curly hairs twining out from between her thighs.

"You're disgusting," she said, and for a second, in the upper left hand corner of the mirror, she saw the movement of a hood, reflected from the second-story window behind her. The Fat Girl had chosen this second story walk-up very deliberately over twenty years ago, thinking the steps would create for her everyday exercise and she would lose weight just by coming home or going out. When she turned from the mirror that night, the real window was empty. The Fat Girl turned off the hallway light and looked outside. She thought she saw Death leaning against the lamppost, his hood turned up toward her.

The next morning, though, he was back at Starbucks, and this time, he beckoned to her. The Fat Girl wished she could avoid him, avoid Starbucks, but the mall was laid out as most malls are, in a big rolling rectangle, and the only way to do the lap was to go all the way around. Even if she didn't do the lap, she had to walk past Starbucks to get to work. When Death beckoned her, one of his fingers stuck out of the end of his sleeve, and he crooked it. She was amazed it didn't appear white and bony. His skin was dark, and even from the distance, and even from only a finger, she got the impression of weight. She ignored him.

He beckoned every day. She ignored him every day. And then, at the end of the week, he not only beckoned, but he had a second cup on the table with him. The Fat Girl knew that it had to be a grande cinnamon dolce latte, her favorite, graced with a small mountain of whipped cream and a sprinkling of cinnamon. Death had even rejected the paper cup and presented her drink in a ceramic in-house mug, which meant it was actually more like a venti in size than a grande. There was a brown paper bag next to it, and the Fat Girl knew it must contain a cheese danish. She hesitated, then walked over.

When she reached the table, Death kicked out her chair, and it slid back just the right amount to let her lower her bulk across from him without bumping into the table and dislodging their drinks. She breathed in the steam, peeked in the bag. She was right.

"You've been missing those," Death said.

The Fat Girl balanced just a bit of whipped cream on her finger and popped it in her mouth, as was her habit. And then she picked up the cup and sipped…and felt the warmth rush through her like a cyclone. The coffee, the cinnamon, the cream, it all whirled into her system and for the first time in weeks, the Fat Girl felt her pulse.

"I've been wanting to talk to you," Death said.

She looked at him over the rim of her cup. Through the hood, she could see a face that looked like it belonged on Easter Island, with features that were long and chiseled and a nose that was flat and out of proportion. But also out of proportion were the cheeks, which were more appropriate for a Buddha. As the Fat Girl swallowed her drink and looked into the heavy eyes, she felt fear bloom in her heart. It fanned out across her breasts and melted down her rolls in streaks of heat.

Standing up, she nearly knocked over her chair, and Death quickly pushed himself back. The Fat Girl deserted her danish, but grabbed her mug and moved as fast as she could down the mall, vowing to bring the mug back to the store later. "Wait!" called Death. But while he could have easily chased the Fat Girl down, he didn't move.

When the Fat Girl arrived at Large & Luscious, she sat down heavily behind the cash register and gulped her latte. "What happened to you?" asked her manager. But the Fat Girl only shook her head. Despite the warm and very real mug between her palms, the Fat Girl still just wasn't sure if Death was real at all. And if he was real, and only she could see him, what did that mean?

Beyond the obvious, which caused her fear to flow again, and puddle at her ankles.

Later that afternoon, as the Fat Girl walked on her break to Starbucks to return the mug, she caught a glimpse of her reflection in a store window. Despite the salads and the fruit, despite the daily morning plod around the mall, she looked exactly the same. "You're disgusting," she said to herself.

At Starbucks, Death's table was empty. The Fat Girl took the mug up to the counter and handed it to the barista. "I'm sorry," she said, "I took this by accident. I was late for work this morning, and I just left without thinking."

The barista smiled. "It's okay, really," he said. "The guy who bought your latte for you paid for the mug. You can keep it. Oh, and here, you left your danish behind. He told us to give it to you."

So The Fat Girl decided to have her mug refilled. She would need something, after all, to wash down her danish. On her way back to the store, she thought about what the barista said. Apparently, she wasn't the only one who could see Death.

But he just kept seeking her out.

Over the next few weeks, the Fat Girl grew increasingly bolder around Death. Every morning, at the end of her lap, he was waiting for her at Starbucks with her latte and her danish. For a while, he had her drink served in paper cups and she just swooped down on him, scooped up her treats, and left. Then he switched back to the ceramic mug, and she sat long enough to sip it down, but still took the danish with her. Finally, one morning, she found not only a ceramic mug, but a matching ceramic plate for her danish. Sighing, still breathing a bit heavily from her exertion, she sank down and decided to stay.

She was halfway through her treat when Death spoke. "So can I talk to you now?" he asked.

Her mouth full, she nodded.

"Okay, look," he said. Leaning forward, his hands emerged from his sleeves and his fingers twined. His nails were finely manicured and she wondered for a moment if they bore a clear polish. "I know what you've been thinking about lately."

The Fat Girl swallowed.

"You've been thinking about…well…me." His hood slid back just a bit and she saw his nose again, the round cheeks. His eyes were deep. "And I just wanted to tell you that you don't have to be afraid."

But Death telling her to not be afraid brought the fear over the Fat Girl again in a sheet. Shoving the rest of the danish in her mouth and snatching her ceramic mug (she would return it later; she doubted he'd pay for another one), she hurried down the mall. Death didn't call after her this time, but when she looked over her shoulder, he was standing by their table, watching her go. His hands were back in his sleeves, and they joined together at his waist, giving him a black angel appearance.

At the store, the Fat Girl wondered why Death seemed so friendly. She worried about it. If he wasn't after her, wouldn't he not pay her any attention at all? Why was he here? He couldn't possibly visit everyone who was afraid of Death; he'd pretty much have to visit the whole world then. Except for those few who called out to him willingly, who wanted release or relief or revenge. But, the Fat Girl mused as she dressed a mannequin in a black and pink tunic, even those few were probably afraid at the last minute. If fear was the issue, then Death would have to see everyone, which just wasn't practical.

So why was he visiting her? Spending so much time?

The Fat Girl placed the pads between the tunic and the mannequin and turned the mannequin into someone who could work in Large & Luscious. For a moment, the Fat Girl wished for the flatness of the plastic skin hiding beneath the tunic; she wished for the smoothness and the hard surface. After tying the sash into a loose bow above the mannequin's newly augmented rear end, which fell off to nothing, just a thin silver pole, the Fat Girl placed her hand on her own chest and felt the steadiness of her heart. The Fat Girl just wasn't ready to go yet.

But then Death showed up at her door. It was late, almost midnight, and the Fat Girl was just getting ready for bed. She was brushing her teeth when she heard the doorbell. Quickly, she covered herself with her robe (she slept in the nude—night sweats made any kind of pajama too hot) and went out to the door. Peeking through the peephole, she saw the hood. She knew it would be Death anyway; no one ever came to visit her, particularly this late at night. Briefly, she thought about just leaving him out there, but then her peephole blurred as he stepped back. Lifting his arms, Death showed her what he was carrying: an extra-large tub of movie popcorn and a blue raspberry slushy. Tucked under his arm was a red and pink bouquet.

The Fat Girl couldn't help it; she smiled. And then she let him in.

Death deposited the snack on the coffee table and the flowers into a vase from the Fat Girl's kitchenette. Then he shucked his coat. Underneath, he wore black jeans and a really nice green and black swirly tie-dyed t-shirt. It reminded the Fat Girl of a hurricane. His arms and legs were full and a soft gut hung gently over his beltline. Despite this, and despite the Easter Island Buddha face, Death was just not unattractive. When he nodded at her and sat down, the Fat Girl sat down next to him. They shared the popcorn, the bucket braced between their thighs, and began passing the slushy back and forth. Their lips and tongues and teeth turned an electric blue.

"I wish you would quit running away," Death said. "I'm not here to hurt you. Or to take you anywhere."

The Fat Girl swallowed. "Then what are you here for?"

Death took up the slushy. "Because I know you're afraid. And I don't want you to be. I don't want anyone to be. See, it's really not a bad thing. Some people even think it's an improvement."

"Yeah, right," she said. "That's why we all work so hard to stay alive."

He shook his head and his tight curls trembled like bed springs. "That's just fear talking," he said and reached out to stroke her cheek.

His touch wasn't cold, as expected. In fact, it was quite warm, slippery with movie popcorn butter and pleasantly scratchy with movie popcorn salt, and the Fat Girl found herself tucking her face into his palm. There was comfort here, and something more. Death graced her face with both hands, not pushing her away, but urging her forward. The Fat Girl leaned in. Her robe gapped open and she scrambled to close it, but his elbows blocked her.

"You're not disgusting," Death whispered, right before he kissed her. His breath mixed with hers and the Fat Girl felt herself sink into a swirl. Instead of moving forward, she moved back, and somehow, they were both impossibly prone on her couch. Death's mouth never left hers, his tongue never stopped its probing slink, as his hands found every curve and crevice that was the Fat Girl. Her robe was gone, his clothes were gone, melted away by the heat of their skins.

The Fat Girl gasped as Death's fingers entered her and she felt herself open in a way she never had before. Instead of turning away, instead of lowering her eyes, she opened them and looked right at him, and saw him looking back. Instead of covering herself with layers, she flung herself exposed and Death offered only his admiration and appreciation. The Fat Girl's body became lithe and slick against Death's, and when he made love to her, it was as if she'd done this before. Many times. Been taken from. Been given to. In between his kisses, Death kept whispering, "You're not disgusting. You're not." And the Fat Girl felt her own body moving in an ancient rhythm and she believed him. She opened her mouth and new sounds came out, so beautiful and agonizing, so full and strangled, and hung in the air like something that had always been there, but was also always missing in her life.

Death stayed the night, and though they moved to the bed, they didn't sleep. As the morning arrived, Death kissed the Fat Girl one final time and said, "See? Death isn't so bad. Imagine what it will be like when you're with me for the long haul." Without seeming to move at all, Death left, his lips leaving behind a warm and moist tattoo circling her left nipple. The Fat Girl looked at his mark, the lip prints slightly open and dark against her skin, and she hoped it wouldn't disappear. She hoped she would see it every time she stood before her full-length mirror.

Before she sunk into sleep, the Fat Girl had the presence of mind to call in sick to work. She wasn't sick at all, and she wanted to call in relaxed...her body had never felt like this before, and yet it felt like it always should have.

The Fat Girl continued to walk the mall, but she also continued to conclude that walk with a treat at Starbucks, sitting at the table she once shared with Death. She dressed with abandon, with bright colors and clingier fabrics, and when men stopped to take in her ample cleavage and curves, she smiled. When she was alone, she enjoyed. When she was with others, she enjoyed. At forty-eight, the Fat Girl decided it was time to join life like jumping off a cliff. Headfirst. Eyes open. Mouth shrieked wide and sucking in air like elixir.

There were no risks. Only Death was waiting. The Fat Girl shimmered with anticipation.

THE FAT GIRL AT THE FAIR

The Fat Girl didn't start out thinking she was going to the state fair. She hadn't been for years, not since she was fourteen years old. Until then, she went with her family, but once she was fully into adolescence, she felt that fair-going should be a dating thing. She wanted to go with a boy. Then a man. One on one. The Fat Girl didn't want to walk singly next to hand-holders, even if they were her friends. She didn't want to walk behind them and have them talk over their shoulders to her, then kiss each other. She wanted to be a hand-holder. She wanted to laugh with her date while they plugged their noses in the cow barn. Look away and blush when the goats mated. Carefully step away from that one fun house mirror that made her look even bigger than she was, though the boy/man she'd be with wouldn't care. He'd wrestle her to the mirror and hold her there and demand she look at herself, really look at herself, and see how lovely she was. And then he'd kiss her, right there in front of everyone, and the kiss would be reflected a million times over, sparkling throughout the funhouse, casting light onto onlookers' faces. So the Fat Girl shook her head at every friend's invitation, every couple's invitation, and waited for this boy, then man, while she stayed at home in her bedroom at her parents' house, and then at her own apartment, watching television. Movies, mostly.

Now thirty-four, the Fat Girl worked as a saleswoman at the Large & Luscious Large Women's Clothing Boutique in the mall. She and the other Fat Girls were all friends there, and when the state fair opened, they gathered around the cash register and talked about it.

"Funnel cake," said one, pretending to drool. "And do you know they sell fried Twinkies and fried peanut butter and jelly sandwiches? They serve them on a stick!"

The only stick food the Fat Girl remembered from the fair was caramel apples. They were topped with chopped nuts. A few times, her apple hit the dirt before she was finished. She always brushed off the gravel and ate it anyway.

"I like the barns," said another. "Those farmers go through so much work, getting their animals ready for the fair. And from babies! They raise them from babies! And then they sell them for food!" She shook her head. "Imagine selling your baby for pork chops or drumsticks."

The Fat Girl always liked the pony rides. She didn't care for the other animals much. She knew what they were there for, and she didn't like to see something looking back at her, flat into her eyes, when she knew it was soon going to be slaughtered.

"For me, the fair's all about the Midway," the manager said. She was sitting at her place behind the counter, and she leaned her head back against her chair and smiled. The Fat Girl always liked the manager's smile, especially when she wasn't talking work. "The roller coasters. The Tilt-a-Whirl. The Matterhorn. Oh, I loved the Matterhorn. They always played great music on that one, and at night, they ran it backwards and had all sorts of flashing lights. It was like a disco on wheels." The manager began to sing softly. "Beep, beep. Beep, beep. The car went beep, beep, beep."

In a theme with the ponies, the Fat Girl supposed, she liked the merry-go-round. Though the ones she liked best had more than ponies. The Fat Girl remembered riding on a chicken. A camel. A dragon. The music was like a calliope, and the canopy above was always mirrored so she could see herself as she went around and around. Just covered in glitter and shine. The Fat Girl never looked at her parents as they waited for her outside the gate. She waved all the way around so that they would think she was watching for them, but she kept her eyes glued to the underside of the canopy, seeing herself and the glitz and a million other children and colors reflected there.

Another salesgirl (it was Friday evening, a traditionally busy night, filled with preparations for the weekend and those customers trying to get a jump on it, and so they had four women working, along with the manager, who would be leaving at six) interrupted the Matterhorn song and said, "So who's going?"

They all glanced at each other. The Fat Girl was the first to answer. "I always thought," she said, "that the fair was a romantic thing. For couples, you know."

The manager waggled her eyebrows and said, "The Tunnel of Love," drawing out the O and deepening her voice.

The Fat Girl looked away.

"The fair is so expensive," said another. "You pay your admission and go in, and suddenly, there goes your whole paycheck. Rides, food, games."

The last nodded. "I have other stuff to do," she said. "Besides, I'm working Saturday and Sunday."

"It has been kind of hot lately," the manager said. But she hummed.

The Fat Girl wandered away. The clothes on clearance for fifty percent off had to be yellow-ticketed down to sixty percent. It always amazed her how well things sold once they were cheaper than half the original price. The other girls went off to do other things. The manager, still humming softly, sat forward to work on the ledger.

The Fat Girl knew what they'd all be doing this weekend, as the state fair went on. While the music played and the cows lowed and the crowd reflected and refracted off funhouse mirrors and merry-go-round canopies, the Fat Girls would all be at home, sitting on their couches, watching television. Movies, mostly.

Funnel cakes, fried Twinkies and peanut butter and jelly sandwiches. She wondered if they still had caramel apples.

So when Saturday came and the Fat Girl had the weekend off and she slept in, then went down to get the mail and felt the sun hit her face, she decided. She went back upstairs, put on a pair of denim capris and a spaghetti strap shirt that was quite a bit daring for a woman of her size, and a comfortable pair of walking sandals. Her toes looked naked, and so she went through the arduous task of bending and painting her nails. Then she plunked sunglasses on her face, stuffed her money and non-maxed credit cards in one pocket, her cell in another, and she left for the bus stop. It would be easier than trying to find a parking space on the fairgrounds. And maybe, she thought, glancing down at her cleavage, there'd be someone to bring her home. She'd always waited for someone to take her to the fair, she realized. She never really considered possibly meeting someone there.

The bus was full when she stepped on, and of course, everyone fell silent. There were only a few open spots, and some of those were window seats and the aisle-sitters didn't look like they were any too ready to move. One seat was quickly covered by a briefcase, but when the Fat Girl paused hopefully, the man sitting next to it was studying his Blackberry. Sighing, the Fat Girl made her way to the most spacious area, near the back doors, and stood, holding onto the pole. Whenever the bus swayed, so did she, and her hips and butt and tummy bumped into the people to her sides, her front, her back. "I'm sorry," she murmured repeatedly, "I'm sorry." Nobody really complained, though the Fat Girl saw a few people lean closer together, shaking their heads, and there were plenty of clustered eyebrows. Once, the guy with the briefcase placed it on his lap to look for something, but when the Fat Girl made a move for the seat, he quickly put the briefcase back down.

When the Fat Girl got off the bus at the entrance to the state fair, she thought she heard a smattering of applause. But, she told herself, it could be coming from one of the sideshows at the Midway.

Walking in, she was swept over with the smells. Popcorn, cotton candy, beer, hot pretzels, nachos. Sweet fought with salt and neither won. They blended and made something totally new, something twisted and yearning and faintly nauseating. The Fat Girl found a caramel apple stand and she bought one and ate it while walking through the game gallery. There were the usuals...skeeball and pennies into fishbowls, balloon-popping with darts, ring a bell with a sledgehammer. "C'mon," the hawker yelled from that one. "You're a big girl, you should be able to send it to the moon!" Onlookers laughed. She thought she heard someone else shout, but she wandered away and pitched a few pennies at goldfish. She won one. She was delighted as a young man handed her a plastic bag filled with water and a shiny orange and red fish.

"Won't make much of a meal for you," the man said, and winked.

The Fat Girl walked carefully, balancing her fish. She wished it came with a bowl. She wondered which was better, to be in a bowl and have pennies plinking and sinking at you all day, or to be stuck in a dark cooler, then pulled out into bright sunshine and hot air and noise that could make its way even through plastic. She wondered how the fish could breathe.

"Hey!" another male voice yelled. "Hey! Over here!" But the words were gruff and so she walked on.

The Midway, the game gallery and the animal barns all met at one central point in the fairgrounds. Someone ingeniously thought to put the pony corral, a combination of farm animal and ride, there. The Fat Girl stopped to watch. She remembered sitting on the ponies, her little sneakered feet slipping into the stirrups. Even though she was instructed to hold the horn, she always held onto the reins, the way a real horsewoman did. A strap went around her waist and held her firmly in the saddle. As all the ponies plodded in their circle, the Fat Girl dreamed of hers transforming into a horse. A mighty palomino. The Fat Girl would shake the reins and her horse would leap forward, crashing through the gate, running through the grounds and out to the meadows and, like the movies, straight into the sunset and the tall masculine shadow that waited there. Buttercup, the Fat Girl called her little pony, whether it was brown or black or white. A few times, she had a pony that shook his head, then bobbed it up and down, and she felt an anticipatory thrill.

Now, she held her goldfish and watched the children go round and round on the backs of ponies. All of them, she noticed, held onto the saddlehorns. One girl had a cowboy hat, but she'd pushed it off her head and it dangled down her back like a fish on a string.

The pony tender, walking around the circle with his ponies, glanced in her direction. "Not a chance," he said.

The Fat Girl moved on. A voice on a megaphone called, "Come here, you'd be perfect! Come back!" The Fat Girl blinked and started to turn, but then she looked down at herself. Her cleavage was wet with sweat, her spaghetti straps slipped down her shoulders. She hadn't been at the fair long, but already her legs felt grimy from the gravel dust. She knew she was far from perfect.

The barns were ahead. She thought about what her co-worker said, about raising the animals from babies to sell as pork chops. The Fat Girl looked at her goldfish and decided she would go in, but just wouldn't look the animals in the eyes.

The chickens and ducks were first, followed by sheep, goats, and cows. The dairy cows were particularly pretty and she stopped to admire them. They must have been bathed because their black and white coats were spotless. A family pushed in next to her, and the kids jostled for position.

"Quite a family resemblance, huh?" the father said.

The cows did all look alike and the Fat Girl glanced at the kids, to see if they noticed, but instead she found them staring at her, nudging each other in the ribs. The father hid his mouth behind his hand.

The Fat Girl walked away, balancing her goldfish. She was hungry again. Food booths were everywhere, touting everything from ribs to pulled pork sandwiches to jambalaya. The Fat Girl remembered when the fair was just hot dogs, hamburgers, cotton candy and caramel apples. Now, the Fat Girl felt inundated with too many choices, and too many things that didn't seem like a fair, but like an expensive outdoor restaurant. Finally, she settled on a burger and a hot dog, corn on the cob dipped in a hot vat of butter and sprinkled generously with salt, and a soda. She promised herself she could have another caramel apple before she left. And maybe she'd try a funnel cake.

But first, there was the matter of logistics. Again, the Fat Girl wished fervently that she was a hand-holder, that there was someone by her side, ready to help her juggle her paper plates, her cup of soda, her goldfish. Instead, there was just the Fat Girl herself, her own two hands, and the goldfish dangling between them.

Looking around at the hawkers, the Fat Girl saw a booth with excruciatingly beaded Indian purses. There was one that she particularly liked, in a pale salmon material, with silver and gold beads glimmering in a spiral. The price was exorbitant, but she bought it anyway, settled it over her shoulder, then eased the fish inside. He was now safe, fully supported, and out of the sun. And so the Fat Girl went to get her meal.

As she ate with her fish at her side, she thought how she just referred to him as male. She didn't know how to tell the gender of fish, but he definitely felt like a he, and she was happy to have him. On the way home, she would stop at the pet store and buy a bowl. Fish food, gravel, red maybe, to coordinate with his color. And some kind of decoration. A castle, a treasure chest. And she had to give the fish a name. Romeo was too obvious. She smiled. Roy, she decided. No one had to know the fish's last name was Mio.

After wiping her mouth and hands, the Fat Girl dumped her trash and took Roy to the bathroom so she could freshen up. Using a damp paper towel, she washed the sweat from her chest and arms, her neck and face. The cool water gave her a rosy glow and she smiled at herself in the mirror. Not bad, she thought, looking again at her cleavage. Not bad for a Fat Girl. She patted the fish at her hip and headed back out to the fair. She decided that it was fun. She might try to win another fish, so Roy could have a friend. Jewel, she already figured. Jewel Ette.

The Fat Girl headed toward the game gallery again, intent on finding the penny fish bowl booth. This time, when the voice came, it was right next to her. "There you are," it shouted, and she startled. Steadying herself, she checked in her purse. Roy was fine, though he seemed a bit shaken. Then the Fat Girl turned to the shouter on her left.

"You're perfect!" he said. "You're perfect!" It was the same voice as before.

She glanced down at herself again and blushed with pleasure.

"Come here," he said, "and play my game. If I lose, I promise you can have any prize in my booth. Any!"

She looked behind him. There were actually some very nice prizes. Jewelry, probably too shiny to be expensive, but pretty. Sweatshirts. Crystal vases. One in particular caught her eye. It was tall and mostly clear, but had a belt of prisms around its middle. The light refracted and she pictured it with red glass beads at the bottom, a tall green plant, and Roy and Jewel, if she won Jewel. She noticed too that the shouter was cute, and about her age. And he thought she was perfect. "Okay," the Fat Girl said. "I'll play your game. What is it?"

He took her arm, quickening her heart, and led her forward. Too late, she saw the giant scale. She started to protest, but the man swung them both around and roared into his spiel.

"Can I guess how much she weighs? How close will I be? What if I'm dead on? If I'm dead on, she walks away with nothing, if I miss by five pounds, she walks away with her choice of prizes! Come test yourself and see how close you are! C'mon! C'mon!"

He yelled and he cajoled and he threatened. He turned the Fat Girl around and around like a prize heifer. People began to gather. Some of them laughed. Others tapped their chins and frowned and figured. A few times, the Fat Girl tried to slip away, but he always cut her off, drew her back, with jeers and a few carefully placed pats. When the crowd had swollen to about twenty-five, the man began to walk around her, pretending to pinch here and there, sizing her between his held-up hands as if she were a model, he, an artist. "Oh, we don't want to add an ounce now, do we," he said, and plucked her bag from her shoulder, her glasses from her nose. He invited her to step out of her sandals, because "I bet this is gonna be a close one!"

The audience began shouting out guesses. Three-fifty! Four-hundred! Six-hundred and ninety-nine! A billion, a child shrieked, and everyone laughed. The Fat Girl tried to smile.

"All right!" the man called, raising his hands for silence. "I will now make my guess. And again…my guess has to be within five pounds in order for me to win. If I am not within five pounds, she takes her choice from the house." Slowly, he again wound around her, bending up and down like an odd carousel horse, though he didn't look like a horse at all. The sun beat down on them both and the Fat Girl felt the sweat bead up and glisten on her chest, sparkle down her arms and legs. She just wanted to grab her fish and run, but there was no way she could. She was caught. The audience would throw her back.

"Okay," the man said. "My guess is…three-hundred and forty-two!"

The Fat Girl shook her head; she knew she didn't weigh that much. But then he cascaded his arms to the scale and asked her to step up. In front of everyone.

"You have to," he said. "Otherwise, we won't know for sure who won."

The crowd cheered for her to go on. "On the scale! On the scale!" they chanted. "Don't break it!" hollered the child and everyone laughed again.

Barefooted, the Fat Girl stepped on the scale. It exploded with a loud groan and everyone roared. The red arrow went crazy, spinning around and around, and then it finally settled. On two-hundred and twenty-one.

The crowd moaned and sighed, and the Fat Girl stepped off. The scale blew whistles. "You've been a good sport," the man said, shaking her hand. "Pick your prize."

Silently, the Fat Girl pointed at the vase. She picked up her bag, made sure Roy was still inside, and slung him on her shoulder. She was stepping back into her sandals when the man handed her the vase, padded with bubble wrap and tucked in a nice paper sack with handles. He returned her sunglasses.

"Thanks," he said. "You were absolutely perfect. Everyone will think I guess badly now, so business will pick up."

As the Fat Girl left the booth, she saw the manager from Large & Luscious standing across the aisle. The Fat Girl broke free from the crowd and the manager joined her, took the bag with the vase from her, and they walked away.

"Well," the manager said. "At least you got a nice prize."

"Thanks," the Fat Girl answered. "I wanted it for my fish. See?" She showed the manager Roy, swimming away in the Indian beaded purse. "I was on my way to see if I could win another one when that man stopped me. And well…" The Fat Girl looked away. "You saw where that went."

The manager shook her head. "Where all have you been?" she asked. "What have you seen?"

The Fat Girl talked about the animal barns and the pony ride, the game galleries and the butter-soaked corn. The manager took her by the elbow and directed her down a different aisle. "I think the fish place is over here," she said. "Then we can go to the Midway."

The fish booth was there, and the young man smiled at the Fat Girl. "Back for another?" he asked. "One not enough for you?"

"A couple would be better, it would keep my fish from being lonely," she said, and did her best to make her voice flirtatious.

He did glance at her cleavage, she noticed, as he handed her twenty pennies for her dollar. So the Fat Girl made sure to bend a lot while throwing. The manager decided to try for a fish too, but she remained fully upright as she tossed, just like the Fat Girl did the first time around. When they were done, the Fat Girl had lost all twenty pennies, but the manager sunk one. The young man gave her a golden fish, with a bright orange cap.

"Here," the manager said, handing the Fat Girl the bag. "You can have her. Then you'll have your couple."

The Fat Girl thanked her and tucked the two fish together. She noticed how they instantly swam toward each other, bumping against their plastic barriers.

Walking through the Midway, the Fat Girl and her manager looked at everything, but didn't ride themselves. They mostly told stories. At the Tilt-A-Whirl, the manager told how, when she was sixteen, she went to the fair with a boy, rode the Tilt-A-Whirl, and then threw up on his lap while giving him a blowjob. He came anyway. By the merry-go-round, the Fat Girl recounted her memories of the chicken, the camel, the dragon, and all the sparkly lights. The roller coaster, the manager said, was the scariest ride of them all, and once, her safety belt came undone right before a big drop. She lived, she said, because of her weight. "If I'd been lighter," she said, "I would have floated out of that seat just like an angel. An angel." She nodded.

They walked around and around, and their elbows bumped into each other, their hips banged, and they laughed. They shared a cotton candy, they both ate a funnel cake and drank iced coffees.

Stopping by the funhouse, the Fat Girl gazed at all the marvelous colors. Reds and oranges, blues and vibrant, violent purples. All sorts of people walked up the ramp, kids, teens, adults. All sizes of adults. "We could do that," she said to the manager.

"Would you like to?" The manager linked her elbow with the Fat Girl's again. "I'm game."

Bags weren't allowed and so the Fat Girl had to leave her vase and the fish, and she was nervous about that. She almost suggested that she and the manager go in separately, but the man taking their money volunteered to watch her things. He tucked everything neatly behind his booth counter. The manager and the Fat Girl went up the ramp and then bounced through multicolored boxing bags. They had to walk over a bridge that had two rows of moving panels, jerking their feet in opposite directions, throwing them off their balance. They put their faces through holes in cut-outs, becoming a carrot, a donkey, a caveman.

By the time they got to the mirrors, they were both breathless and sweaty from laughing. The first mirror that the Fat Girl stood before made her into a zigzag. The next stretched her to over seven feet tall. In the third, she suddenly squashed down like an accordion. And then the fourth one came, and the Fat Girl began to quickly step away.

"Stop," the manager said. She joined the Fat Girl.

They stood there, two blobs in the mirror, their edges blurred, their bodies blended. The manager put her arm around the Fat Girl's waist, she leaned her head on the Fat Girl's shoulder, and the two of them became one large breathing wobble-edged creature. "Look," the manager said. "See? How beautiful. Our kind has to stick together." As the manager stepped away, her hand trailed over and around the Fat Girl's hips, and she thought she felt the manager's lips briefly on her shoulder.

The Fat Girl's insides went as wobbly as the reflection.

It wasn't what she wanted. It wasn't what she planned or dreamed of, as she sat at home, watching movies, and thinking about couples and state fairs. But still. It felt good. No longer laughing, she stepped away, and when the manager offered her hand, she took it and followed her out of the funhouse.

They collected the fish, then had dinner in one of the shelters. The Fat Girl decided to try ribs, but had corn on the cob again, and the manager had nachos and french fries and apple cider. They juggled each other's plates, balanced cups and made it without a spill. They listened to a band for a while, then headed for the gates. The manager had her car with her, and the Fat Girl gratefully accepted the ride. They stopped at a pet store, bought red glass beads and a live green plant, fish food and a treasure chest. The clerk warned the Fat Girl that state fair fish didn't usually live very long, but she decided not to listen. This was Roy and Jewel. They would live. They met at the fair. They were hand-holders.

At the manager's apartment, the Fat Girl decided to go ahead and set the vase up, to let the fish out of their bags. The manager sat on a barstool and watched. The overhead light caught the prisms, setting off a curve of gleam and glisten, and the fish added sparkles of red and orange and gold as they swam around and around.

When the manager gave the Fat Girl a tour of the apartment, led her into the bedroom and kissed her on her lips, the Fat Girl wasn't sure what to do. But when the manager lowered the spaghetti straps, raised the Fat Girl's breasts as reverently as if a host and chalice at communion, and then lowered her mouth to them, the Fat Girl gave in. She learned the meaning of swoon and she sunk to the bed and turned her head toward the closet, toward the mirrored doors. She watched the sparkle of light as she felt herself refracted by the softest of strokes, the glisten of tongue and lips, and the rise and fall and round and round of her own body. The taste, the sound, the salt, the silk of skin and hair, curves and valleys, were everywhere. Reflected into a thousand sighs in the manager's eyes and in the Fat Girl's heart.

Afterward, holding hands, the manager said, "See? Our kind should stick together."

The Fat Girl breathed easily and floated. From the kitchen, there was, every now and then, the soft chink as the exuberant fish created enough wake to bounce a glass bead. The Fat Girl thought about sticking together, about kinds, the way the cows stood side by side, or her fish bounced off opaque walls to see each other. She thought of children on ponies and merry-go-rounds, looking up into their faces reproduced a million times over and sparkled with glee and glass. The Fat Girl looked over at the manager and thought of kind.

"How much did you think I weighed?" the Fat Girl asked the manager. "Did you guess?"

"I didn't," the manager said. "Babe, I was only looking at you. Do you know how lovely you are?"

The Fat Girl glanced at the mirror, at the two of them reflected there, their hands interlaced tightly between pressed and overlapping thighs. The fish clinked in the kitchen and she sighed and felt the bed begin to move, to spin, slowly at first and then faster. In the reflection, her face shattered into millions of faces, blending smiles and eyes and noses into a kaleidoscope of pink and red and blue. And the manager too, calling her name, her voice mixing in and undulating over her body. They joined. They joined and they blurred and the Fat Girl swooned. Around and around, in the glimmer and shine of skin and soft and sex, the Fat Girl swooned. Her fingers never let go.

THE FAT GIRL INSIDE

You always have a secret in your pocket. It travels from your jeans to your slacks to your skirt to your shirt. When you wear a smooth-fitting dress, you tuck the secret into your bra, and if there's no bra, then into your panties. You've even been known to stick it between your heel and your shoe, when you have to. Your secret always presses against your skin somewhere, a tactile reminder, except when you sleep. Then, it rests on your dresser, propped up by your mirror. You stand there, before bed and first thing in the morning, and you let your eyes slide from your reflection, to the secret, to the reflection, to the secret.

There are moments when you look around, admire what you have now. Sleek and clingy clothes. Your closet is a jungle of bright color. Your hair is well done, well cared for, slinking around your ears and nape in a way that looks easy, but isn't. You have a new job, so different from the one you used to have. And there are the men. It is no longer rare to get men into your bed. A certain walk, a certain blink, a particular drop to your voice, and they no longer just look, but take action. You remember when the looks were stares, and not at all like what you get now. The stares used to spear you, slice you up, throw you away as heavy confetti. Now, men's eyes skim your body with the promise of fingertips, stopping here, then there, and create a special heat that you used to only know from rented movies. Rented, because you didn't used to fit in theater seats.

Your life is so different now. But your secret reminds you that this is just exterior camouflage. Your life is different, but inside, you are still the same. Inside, you are still the Fat Girl.

Your secret, a photograph. Taken the very first time you slipped away on your lunch hour from your old job as a sales clerk at the Large & Luscious Large Women's Clothing Boutique in the mall. Instead of going to eat that day, like you told your co-workers, you turned the corner, rode down the escalator, and went into the backroom at Sears, where mall employees were invited to attend a diet program's weekly classes. You filled out forms, leaving your weight blank (you really didn't know, you didn't own a scale), your age blank (none of their business), your height a lie (two extra inches, so when you did weigh in, it wouldn't look so bad). A thin golden lady, yellow fitted suit, blonde upswept hair, yellow open-toed stilettos, chunky gold jewelry, took your forms and walked you to the scale, hidden behind a screen. The scale was digital, and as you stepped on, you watched the numbers fly by like ticker tape, 100, 200, 300. Then the numbers slowed. And stopped. And next to the golden lady, you were bright red. The red of wine that you wouldn't drink for months. The red of a tomato that you would soon eat alone and call it lunch, feeling guilty when you sprinkled it with a little salt.

The golden lady said nothing, just wrote your ticker tape number down, then backed you against a beige wall. She took your secret and gave it back to you. You've kept it with you ever since. She wrote your weight again in a little booklet which she folded into three sections, slid into a plastic pouch, and handed to you. The booklet became your bible, something you opened repeatedly during the day and sometimes in the middle of the night, to look at your weight loss. To pray over it. To have faith in it. The way the numbers dropped. You will always remember the day that 203 switched to 199.5. The battle wasn't over with yet, but you were triumphant. You couldn't remember the last time your weight began with a 1.

But you do remember what it was like, before that red day. You can see your secret, even with your eyes closed. The chins that hid your neck. Your breasts like faulty cannonballs, resting to the left and the right of a stomach that tried to grab everyone's attention. The way your arms didn't go straight down, but were shoved away by breasts and belly, your hands dangled over hips. Your fingers like hot dogs. Fat little finger hot dogs, curling toward an impossible body. A body you hated. And a body you know is still inside.

You are slim now, you see it in your reflection. But around you, the air hesitates, remains at a distance, enclosing you in a bubble of expectation…one mistake, two, and your body will explode that bubble, take up all the air that refuses to believe in your loss. Refuses to believe in you.

The mistakes. You've made some, but you've caught them. So far. On a dinner date, the waiter asked if you'd like dessert, and you were having so much fun, laughing and drinking and flirting, that you exclaimed yes and ordered a hot fudge sundae, tasting every word. Then you shuddered and asked for two spoons, and let your date eat it all, except for one spoonful that you dipped in and out of your mouth, for show. Another day, running late for work at your new job, Large & Luscious far behind you now, you threw an energy bar into your purse, but the growl of your stomach forced your car into a fast food drive-through. Trapped by cars, you couldn't escape, and you were nearly in tears when you reached the microphone. The aroma of the place, the eggs, the bacon, the cheese, biscuits more butter than flour, wrapped around you like a hug, like a noose. When the static voice asked you what you wanted, you thought coffee, but you ordered an entire breakfast, your old usual, with juice, and you paid and drove off with it. It sat in your passenger seat like succulent dynamite and you stopped at the closest garbage can and dumped it. But not without taking one bite of the egg and sausage and cheese sandwich. Just one bite. You kept the orange juice, skipped the energy bar at work. You survived.

But you know what could happen, you know your secret is shallow. So you keep it with you at all times. Touching you at all times. Except at night, when you sleep. Then the secret stares at you from your dresser, backed by your empty mirror.

Your new job is in advertising. You are finally able again to take advantage of your degree, to do what you are trained to do, what you love. When you were fired years ago, the company said it was because of a snafu with a project, but you knew it was your size. They never looked at your face anymore. They stared at the way your thighs and ass bulged out of the too-small desk chair in your little cubbie, a cubbie made even smaller by the enormity of you. Fired, fat, you couldn't go anywhere, and you ended up a sales clerk at Large & Luscious, where they welcomed you, the Fat Girls, where you fit in, and for a while, it was okay. But there was so much flesh. The thermostat, always turned low in the store, couldn't combat the heat rising from overstuffed skin, couldn't stop the chafing and rubbing and friction and salt and smell. And so the weight loss meetings.

When you got down to 140 pounds, you left Large & Luscious, you left behind the Fat Girls who watched you go with full and hungry eyes. You don't go back for friendly catch-up visits. The Fat Girls know the secret you keep in your pocket. At 120, you bought a yellow suit, just like the golden lady's, and you interviewed for a job in advertising, and you got it. They saw your smile. You bared your teeth. You hid the sucking hole inside of you that still clamored.

You feel your skin stretch. Full to bursting.

Working late into the night on a project, you look up finally to realize you are all alone. The janitor turned off the overhead lights long ago, and only your computer and desk lamp throw illumination, your cubbie a spotlight in the dark. You glance at the lower right corner of your screen; eleven o'clock. You haven't eaten since your green salad, topped with two ounces of skinless chicken breast and one tablespoon of fat-free dressing, at lunch. The golden lady preaches eating often, preaches eating at least five small meals a day, and you can picture her, sitting on your shoulder, knees neatly crossed, stilettos dangling, and she shakes a skinny finger at you. You are entering a danger zone, she says. You need to eat something healthy, step back from that edge of hunger.

You haven't planned ahead, and that is another mark against you. The golden lady frowns. You push back your chair, the chair you fit into so well, and walk through the dark aisles to the employee break room. Leaving the fluorescents off, you cross to the refrigerator and open it. The white light inside falls out and sears through you, your head above it, your feet below. It goes right through your middle, through your yellow suit, your belt tugged to the fifth hole, the tail neatly slid through a loop. The light crystals float in the air. And then you duck in, the coldness hitting you full in the face. Like a slap. A slap to the unconscious to become aware. A slap to the hysterical to calm down.

It's amazing what people leave behind.

There is a co-worker's remaining half of a sub sandwich. The salami and ham glisten with mayo. There are one, two, three, four, five containers of yogurt. An opened baggie of trail mix. Three cups of vanilla pudding, one of butterscotch. A Tupperware with its lid partway burped off, the scent of a pasta salad glittering the air. Bottom shelf, the remains of an executive's birthday cake from the best bakery in town. Marble. Mocha frosting. There is fruit too, so much of it, peaches and apples and pears and even a sliced pineapple.

Who knows how old it all is? In this light, to your eyes, it is young. And there is nobody else here.

Your hand trembles as it reaches for an apple. You bite into the red skin, expose the white, the crunch loud, and your eyes find the cake. You let your hand drop casually while you chew, and the apple, oh so easily, grazes the cake, comes up with frosting smeared on its virgin white. And you bite.

And then you kneel. Immersed in the light of the fridge, you kneel and you embrace and it all reaches for you.

All of it.

Your belt goes first, undone, dangling, then falling to the floor. Your jacket next, the two buttons pinched, the gasping absolution when they fly open, the jacket tumbling off your shoulders, and it's gone. Skirt unclasped, unzipped, puddles lifeless to the floor. The cold light sparks your black cami, the lace a filigree against your cleavage, and your panties, silky wisp suddenly tight, and then they're gone too. Nothing holds you in now. You are burgeoning. You are free.

And your secret too, from the pocket of your skirt, falls free. No longer touching you. But effervescing into the air.

You eat. You eat and you sob with the release of it, the pure emancipation, the absolute deliciousness of taste and texture and filling, filling, filling. The stretch of your skin, the widening of your throat, your stance, your legs, your arms, your eyes, you eat. You eat and you eat and you gorge.

And then the fridge is empty. You are gap-jawed, bleary-eyed, your body speckled with crumbs and dollops, plastic and saran surround you. Slumping to the floor, you roll to your side, and then your back. You can still smell it all. You can smell it inside you.

Where you know it will rot. You know you will rot. Rot in liberation, in lack of care, lack of worry, lack of life. Freedom.

You think of getting up on hands and knees, crawling to the trashcan, throwing up. Correcting the mistake. But your eyes close.

Early the next morning, they find you there, exposed. Spread on the floor like roadkill in a headlight, the white of the light and the cold of the air throwing you, throwing your secret into their faces.

They stare, spear you, then turn away.

You stand up, close the fridge door, cover yourself with your unbuttoned skirt, your clutched-together jacket. You leave without stopping at your desk. Abandoning your purse that still has your energy bar. That has your tri-folded bible, the numbers sinking down, encased in plastic.

You leave your secret on that floor, scattered with your remains and crumbs. They all know it now anyway.

You know it too.

The golden lady, slipped from your shoulder long ago, crawls into your purse and dies.

You go home. To your empty bed that will stay empty, to a closet that will soon be filled with a chaos of clothes that don't fit. You lay down naked, sprawl on the mattress, toss away the negligee from your last date. Your very last date.

You will go to the mall tomorrow. They will greet you, the Fat Girls at Large & Luscious, with open arms that dimple and crease. Their eyes will no longer be full and hungry, but sad and unsurprised.

They knew your secret all along.

They knew it was never a secret.

You sleep, exposed to the world.

FAT GIRL OUTSIDE

The Fat Girl kept her private world miniature because she was anything but. Every morning, she shuffled around her apartment and adjusted all of the rooms in a dozen dollhouses, moving couches in the Victorian living room, then setting a table in the Colonial, then transforming a child's bedroom into an art studio, a dining room/living room combo into a ballroom. In her own kitchen, the Fat Girl maneuvered her collection of tiny tea sets, arranging and rearranging the cups so that hundreds of fairy guests would have their share of tea. In the living room, she looked in a minuscule mirror, filled with only her mouth as she put on lipstick. She turned over two tiny hourglasses, one brass, one wooden, and checked the time on her miniature mantel clock. Eight-thirty. All this before she left for work in the Large & Luscious Large Women's Clothing Boutique in the mall.

The Fat Girl hated her job which she took because she thought she blended in which was why she hated it. Everything there was gigantic. Sizes 24, 36 and 48. XL, 2XL, 3XL, 4, 5, and 6XL until the idea of so many X's made her eyes cross. There were shirts that promised to button down, but always gapped open. Pants whose pleats claimed to hide baggy bellies, but cradled them like unborn babies. Underwear that could flap for surrender in the wind. And girdles that lured women in with the promise of never having to come to a store like this again. Her customers bought scores of these, then flew out with large pink plastic bags, secure in the promise that once the girdle slid over their soft thighs and hips and squeezed in their stomachs in an attempt to find a waistline, they could cross the hall and shop at the Petite Sophisticate. The Fat Girl never tried these girdles on. She never bought one. She wasn't blind.

But even the Fat Girl glanced over at the Petite Sophisticate on her lunch breaks as she sat alone on the bench outside her store. She no longer ate in the food court; the tables were too small and the looks were too long. So she pulled things out of fast food bags one by one and chewed and thought about going from Luscious to Sophisticated. Luscious. She looked down at her body, spread like an unbaked loaf of bread on the bench. Luscious was only in the name because it started with an L. Large and Lard-Ass Women's Boutique just wouldn't sell.

But at home, in her miniature world, the Fat Girl could be Sophisticated too. She looked in the dollhouse rooms and spoke out loud about the fairness of the weather, the social events for the evening, the latest promotion or beau or dalliance. Her voice was high and soft and the accent changed as she bobbed from house to house, just a hint of British or gentle southern belle or the lilt of French which she took years ago in high school. She spoke for the dolls in her bedroom too, each having a distinct and refined voice. She turned the hourglasses over every time she strolled by. And she tilted her head, wherever she was, to listen to the delicate sound of the miniature mantel clock chiming the hour.

And she did all this naked. Sophisticated People walked around their homes nude, she assumed. They came home from their high-power, business-suit, do-lunch-eat-salad jobs and they stripped, putting their clothes in wicker and brass laundry hampers, the dry-clean-onlies on padded and scented hangers in their closets. Sophisticated People sighed as the air returned to their exposed, slim, beautiful bodies, their skin reflecting gold in the evening light flickering in the garden window, or rosy pink in the warm glow from the brick and marble fireplace. Sophisticated Women stretched agile cat limbs on black leather sofas and they sipped martinis from crystal stemware. Sophisticated Men stood by the home bar, their sculpted genitals rock hard as they shook another martini for themselves. Sophisticated Women watched and desired.

The Fat Girl did this too, although she had to imagine the genitals. She sprawled naked on her brown corduroy sectional, trying and failing to keep both legs on the cushions at the same time. She drank a light beer and wondered what a martini tasted like. How could something wet be dry? She thought they might taste like Arizona air.

At home or at work, Sophisticated or not, the Fat Girl avoided mirrors, in the bathrooms or the dressing rooms, the front windows of the stores in the mall, or even the minuscule mirror that she used for lipstick. A few dollhouses had mirrors as well and the Fat Girl stood in such a way that no part of her ever reflected.

When it came to slimming down, the Fat Girl tried it all. Slimfast. Weight Watchers. Jenny Craig. Gyms and wraps and hypnosis. She liked the hypnosis, it made her very relaxed, but her hunger never went away. She came home from each appointment, stretched out on the couch, every bone and muscle loose, and ate a bucket of ice cream.

But she tried.

One afternoon, after lunch, she lumbered down the mall to All Things Remembered, a gift shop. She loved it there, although the close aisles and breakables made her very anxious. After many trips, she planned out the best path possible for someone of her girth and she followed it each time, until she ended up in front of a glass cabinet filled with miniatures. This was payday and depending on the sales, she could pick out one or more.

She stood there and pondered, her arms pressed tightly against her sides. There was a blue china cabinet she liked, complete with tiny plates and saucers and cups hanging on hooks. It would go well in the Country Dollhouse's kitchen. There was also a clawfooted bathtub and a little toilet, complete with a tank hanging above it with a pull chain. Her Victorian Dollhouse didn't have a bathroom yet. She debated back and forth for a while, wondering which house was more important, which was closer to completion, and then she decided to splurge. It was payday, she had no plans for the weekend, what the hell.

She went to the cash register and told the clerk what she wanted. She watched the girl go through the curtain to the back room, where all the lovely things were kept boxed up. The Fat Girl noticed the snug-waisted dress, the slim legs, the ankles that looked oh so chic in strappy red slingbacks. She looked at her own brown loafers, soles worn down on the inside, giving her heels a tilted look, her body knock-knees. When the clerk returned, she handed over the boxes for inspection and the Fat Girl noticed a large diamond on the skinny left hand. The Fat Girl quickly peeked in the boxes and nodded. "These are fine," she said softly.

Back at Large & Luscious, the Fat Girl found all the other girls in a huddle around several huge cardboard cartons. "Look at these!" one called and the Fat Girl joined in, lifting a long and narrow pink box. On the front was an undoubtedly large woman, but she was also curvaceous and sleek in a full and round way. Inside the box was a long, one-piece body shaper. When the Fat Girl held it up, it flowed from her neck to her ankles.

"It trims everything!" one of the other girls said.

"Get a display set up," said the manager. "Put one on a mannequin."

The Fat Girl went to deposit her things in the back room, then joined another girl by a large squat podium. The girl was quickly stacking the body shaper boxes, so the Fat Girl dressed the mannequin. While the mannequin was large, the Fat Girl always noticed how she wasn't that large. She wondered if customers really thought that a body shaper could change the way a mannequin looked. If they thought that a body shaper could change the way a woman looked.

And yet, by three o'clock, the Fat Girl lost count of how many pink boxes she put into pink bags. As the afternoon and evening wore on, she held each purchase a bit longer, looked at it more closely. With her employee discount, it would only cost her forty-nine dollars. Which was less than the miniatures, both of them, combined. If it worked. The Fat Girl doubted it, but she hesitated more and more as she looked into the eager eyes of her customers and listened to their excited chatter. By closing, the Fat Girl noticed not a single body shaper had been returned and so she moved a little slower, studying the curvaceous woman on the slim boxes as she bagged them for each of her co-workers. Everyone else bought one. Even the manager.

It was the Fat Girl's weekend off which meant she was the Friday night closer. She stayed after everyone else, balancing the cash register drawers, straightening up, locking the doors. She stopped and looked at what was left of the body shaper display. The delivery cartons were empty and collapsed in the back room and there were so few pink boxes left, the Fat Girl couldn't even make a pyramid. She formed what she thought was an artful display, the body shapers spinning in a domino row, just one touch would send them falling. She glanced through the front windows and saw that the mall was empty, the lights dimmed. The security guard wouldn't even know she was here. Carefully, her fingers poised, she snatched the front body shaper and took it to the dressing rooms.

Selecting number eight, a number she always thought was lucky and the size she secretly wanted to be, the Fat

Girl shut the door firmly behind her. With her back to the mirror, she undressed, then pulled the body shaper from its box.

Stepping into it was like pulling on a spandex noose. The Fat Girl grunted as she pulled it over one thick calf and thigh, then the other. It went over her backside first, then she yanked it over her stomach and she gasped as she felt herself squeezed. She tucked one arm into a strap and pulled until her right breast was squashed, then the other strap came up and her lungs compressed.

Stiffly, her body encased in white elastic (why not pink, she wondered, to match the box?), she stepped back into her clothes. Her pants did feel looser, her blouse didn't gap. She allowed herself one moment to wonder. One moment to wish.

But when she held her breath and turned to look quickly in the mirror, she knew she still couldn't walk across the hall and browse through the racks. She still wasn't Sophisticated.

She turned her back again and pulled her clothes off. When she lowered the straps of the body shaper, her breasts heaved out and down like the waves of the ocean and she could breathe a little easier. She loosened her body, roll upon roll, peeling the shaper down. But as she stepped out of one leg, her ankle caught and she tripped. Twisting sideways, trying to catch herself, she rotated and braced herself on the mirror.

And there she was.

Bent over, elastic halfway up one leg and bunched around the ankle of the other. Breasts folded together and wobbling, backdropped by a pockmarked swaying stomach which was framed by two creased thighs. Her arms, flabby wings holding her body up, flapped.

The Fat Girl shuddered and her body rolled in a huge tidal wave of weight. She felt it pour from her shoulders to her toes and suddenly her legs were too heavy to lift.

She felt cemented to the floor, standing there, looking in the mirror, the body shaper crumpled and useless at her feet. Body shaper, she thought. Something to shape this into a body. This mountain. Not mountain. This slag-heap.

She turned slowly and dressed. She kicked the body shaper into the corner, then sent the box spinning after. Grabbing her miniatures, she left. She glanced over at the darkened petite shop, its windows filled with mannequins with no heads, but slender exquisite bodies, clothes clinging, curves and hollows so delicate and lovely. She thought for a moment of putting her hands around those tiny waists, just to see what the sharp bone of ribs felt like, the gentle swelling out of hips and breasts, instead of following formless curves that went forever out and out and out.

She passed the security guard. She saw him glance at her and look away.

On the way home, she began to panic. The seat of her car was thrust all the way back, yet still the steering wheel dug into her stomach. She felt enclosed and she cracked the window to let in some air. She stopped at the grocery store and roamed the health and diet aisles, looking for something new, something untried, a clinically proven miracle, but there were none. She put Slimfast in her basket, then took it out. She put Metabolife in her basket, then took it out. She began to gasp. There was nothing new, nothing here at all. As fast as she could, she stumbled over to the produce section and threw grapefruit in the basket, lettuce, more grapefruit, bananas, then already sliced and peeled carrot sticks and celery.

But she'd already tried it all. She knew the lettuce would grow limp and brown, the grapefruit would turn soft and eventually the whole dripping, moldy mess would have to be scooped out of her refrigerator, and she would chide herself for spending wasted money, hate herself for failing. Tears became trapped in the folds around her eyes. Abandoning her basket, she left the store.

At home, she stripped and her body rolled out over itself, skin against skin, and she felt the relief of freedom. She skipped her beer and sat on the couch, putting the two new boxes of miniatures on her coffee table.

She looked around at her miniature world, so small, so neat. In the dollhouses, the tiny families sat on sofas in front of televisions or radios or nothing at all. Some slept in beds while others cooked in tiny kitchens. The wrists of these little people, the ankles and necks, so thin and fragile, they could be snapped with a bend of the Fat Girl's fingers. As she well knew, from many mishaps when her fingers were just too thick and clumsy for what she wanted to do.

Yet the dollhouse people were all so beautiful. Their delicacy was sharp and refined. Sophisticated.

The Fat Girl leaned forward and watched as her elbows sank into the soft padding of her thighs.

She looked in the kitchens of the dollhouses and she wondered what the tiny people were eating. If they ate lettuce and grapefruit. If they drank diet shakes and swallowed pills. Closing her eyes, she pictured herself newly thin, just as delicate, just as beautiful, in the dollhouse kitchens. But all she saw behind her eyelids was the dressing room mirror full of trembling flesh.

The miniature mantel clock chimed eleven. The sound reminded her that she hadn't eaten. In answer, her stomach rumbled.

The Fat Girl started for her own kitchen, but then she stopped and looked back. The miniature people were there, living out lives so tiny and perfect, the men handsome, the children smart, the women with snug-waisted dresses and diamonds on their fingers. She wondered. She reached for something she hadn't tried.

Opening one of the new boxes, she pulled out the new miniature china cabinet. She set it aside and found the little plates and cups and saucers, all individually wrapped in bubbles. One by one, she opened them, then placed each piece in her mouth. The sound was delicate between her teeth.

She moved to the dollhouses and began picking out the people, placing them limb by limb in her mouth. Arms and legs, heads and torsos. Each impossibly small, each too tiny to taste. She took them in and felt herself growing smaller.

She moved to her kitchen, picking out the tiniest of teacups and tasted rose petals and gold filigree, green leaves and silver scrolls. When the clock chimed eleven-thirty, she returned to the living room. Turning the clock around, she opened the back and looked in at the miniature workings. She carried the clock to the couch, sat down, and began to pick through and graze.

With each swallow, her body shrank. She could feel it happening. She chewed or swallowed whole until she couldn't anymore, her eyes closed, in her mind the image of herself stepping up to the dollhouses, stepping in, taking the place of the families at the radio, or soaking her tiny body in the new clawfooted tub. She saw herself sleeping in the pink canopied bed, her body lost in the silk sheets and soft pillows. In the morning, she would get up, slip soundlessly to the ground, and go to work, where she would hand in her resignation. They would all stand amazed and applaud as she crossed the hall of the mall to the other store. To the world of Sophistication, the world where waists nipped in and breasts curved out, yet hung proudly high.

Her stomach felt tight. The way it was supposed to feel, her skin snug against sharp hipbones and ribs. Slowly, she leaned to the right and wrapped her arms around herself as she fell into the embrace of the couch. Her breath came easier as she entered this new world, her body floating and impossibly light, and she smiled and felt the lift and stretch of her sharp and prominent new cheekbones. Her world shrank into one tiny black hole. Lifting her arms over her head, her new body poised and taut on the edge, the Fat Girl dove in.

THE FAT GIRL STRIDES HIGH

The Fat Girl really didn't know why she wanted to go to the Grand Canyon. She didn't ever go on vacation. When she was forced by corporate to take time off of work, from the Large & Luscious Large Women's Clothing Boutique in the mall, she spent it at home. She would sleep late. Sometimes until noon. She went to the city zoo or to a museum or to the movies. It was always a relief and a joy to get back to the boutique. She loved the consistency and riot of the fabric around her, and the consistency of the women who came in looking for clothes to make them beautiful, and left feeling that they were. She enjoyed the conversations she shared with the other Fat Girls, and with the way they could communicate when necessary in absolute silence. A raised eyebrow meant that a customer was approaching racks of clothes totally different from those she currently wore. A scowl meant the customer was a browser and would walk out empty-handed. And a big smile meant a big sale was on the way and someone should rescue the customer from her armload of clothes (empty arms meant they could be filled again) and set up a dressing room. There were a variety of other looks too, to cover the multitude of attitudes and appearances of Large & Luscious customers.

One day in early November, the manager issued a warning to the Fat Girl, that she still had two weeks of vacation to use by the end of the year. Large & Luscious was generous, but firm with their vacation policy; their employees had to give themselves some time off. Period. The manager wasn't too happy that the Fat Girl had waited until this late in the year as they were about to launch into the busy holiday season. The Fat Girl wasn't happy either and groused all the way to the food court for her lunch break. She'd hoped, with the arrival of November, that corporate might have forgotten about her and her unused days. But Big Fat Sister, as the Fat Girl and her co-workers liked to call corporate, always had an eye out for them. The Fat Girl supposed she should be appreciative.

It was near the end of her lunch hour that the Fat Girl overheard a conversation. It probably started earlier, but the Fat Girl was engrossed in her new book, picked up on clearance from Barnes & Noble. A heavy collection of classic poetry, and it cost her less than three dollars. She was in the middle of Emily Dickinson's "Because I Could Not Stop For Death" when a chorus of giggles interrupted her.

Four other shopgirls sat close together at the table beside the Fat Girl. She noticed three were eating salads and one was chewing a bagel. They all wore really expensive clothes; the Fat Girl recognized the styles from the mall's high-end stores. She liked walking through those stores, seeing the lovely colors and fitted styles, and imagining them someday on her own body. She didn't kid herself; she never thought she would one day buy these particular clothes from these particular stores. Their fashions tended to make their way in similar styles and colors, but different cuts to Large & Luscious. The Fat Girl always waited for them there, rejoicing when they appeared like old friends in new stock.

The four shopgirls in the food court ate and giggled and their clothing shimmered. The Fat Girl took quick and cautious glances and detected their ID badges. Their names were indecipherable from the Fat Girl's distance, but she could see the stores' names. Sure enough, Saks and Macy's. But also Chico's and White House/Black Market. The Fat Girl finished her pizza and pretended to read her book while she eavesdropped. She conjectured the girls' names from their piping voices and sharp laughter. Kristi. Ashley. Mindy. And for the Chico's girl, something exotic, like Sahara. The Fat Girl smiled.

Then White House/Black Market mentioned the Grand Canyon. Her voice deepened, glowed with reverence, and the Fat Girl tilted her head to hear better. "It was so big," the shopgirl said. "I mean, it was bigger than big. There's not even a word for it. You can't even believe it's real when you see it. And ohmygod, so beautiful."

The other girls leaned in and pressed for more details, but then they bopped on to Saks' vacation in Hawaii. The Fat Girl noticed that White House/Black Market didn't say anything else. She ate her salad slowly and her eyes were unfocused. As if she was still there. Still seeing all of that big beauty. She ate as if she were in a dream.

The Fat Girl looked down at herself. She was sitting at the handicapped table because it had a moveable chair that she could adjust for her size. She always told herself she would move instantly if she was approached by a shopper in a wheelchair, but in ten years, that had never happened.

Big, the dazed shopgirl said. Bigger than big. And beautiful.

The Fat Girl looked down again, and then over at the other table. The girls wore bright colors and so did she. All the fabrics were rich and flowing. The only thing different, the Fat Girl thought, was her size. And the belts they wore cinched tight around their waists. The shopgirls were tiny, the largest size among them, the Fat Girl guessed, a six. The Fat Girl was a twenty-four. Yet they were considered beautiful. The Fat Girl was just big.

But the Grand Canyon was unspeakably big. And unspeakably beautiful.

So the Fat Girl decided she had to go. It was the beginning of November and she had two weeks of vacation to use up and she'd be back before Thanksgiving and Black Friday and the holiday rush. It would even make the manager happy. And Big Fat Sister. The Fat Girl could probably leave by this weekend.

She wanted to come back as dazed as White House/Black Market. Dazed at the sight of big and beautiful. She wanted to see what it looked like.

The trip was easy to arrange and she took off on Saturday morning. She decided to take a direct flight to Phoenix, and then drive the rest of the way, giving her a chance to see some of the sights. She'd never been to the southwest and she'd heard it was hot, which worried her since she found heat intolerable. But it was November, so how hot could that be? Plus all references to Arizona always included the phrase, "dry heat." The Fat Girl wasn't sure what that was supposed to mean, but everyone always sounded like a dry heat was okay. The Grand Canyon itself, she read, was supposed to be chilly this time of year, possibly even cold enough to snow.

She booked a cabin for a week, figuring she could either extend her stay into the second week, or decide to travel to other sights. The cabin was on the south rim, so she would be right within the park, right within sight of the canyon. The name of the resort entranced her: Bright Angel. Bright, Big and Beautiful Angel, she paraphrased.

The flight was pretty easy. She had an aisle seat and she read her poetry book with her arms tucked in tightly so as not to disturb anyone. She only got up to use the restroom once, and she accompanied her hip-bumping walk down the aisle with a chorus of "sorries," and smiles. At the car rental counter, the clerk did a double-take and the Fat Girl saw him scratch something out on her paperwork. He offered her a roomy sedan and she accepted it. When she got into the car, she glanced at the paperwork and saw that he'd crossed out "compact."

It was eleven o'clock in the morning in Phoenix and it was wonderfully warm. Not oppressive at all. The Fat Girl reveled in being able to lower the car's window and let the breeze come in and play through her hair and down her body. Her winter coat was safely stowed in the back seat, her suitcase in the trunk. The GPS said that it was around a three-hour trip to the canyon.

At first, the drive seemed like a typical cruise through a metropolitan area. But then, all of a sudden, the city just dropped away. It was like a line had been crossed, a border that said, the city is on this side, and over here is the desert. It was like driving through a lanai. The Fat Girl found herself chugging up mountains, flying down them. The mountains were dark, grays and browns and blacks, and the landscape was barren with just a few green plants scattered here and there. The cacti really did look like the Saturday morning cartoons the Fat Girl used to watch when she was a child. They stood erect, headless bodies, waving handless arms to Heaven. The Fat Girl wanted to stop, to see if they were really as prickly as they looked in Hanna-Barbera, but she was terrified to pull over. The traffic moved swiftly on these inclines and the Fat Girl, once outside of her car, didn't.

Then the colors began. The mountains fell into richness and by the time she hit Sedona, the red was astounding. Formations bounded and surged out of the ground like airborne lava and the Fat Girl stopped at a service station so she could pick up an information map. The formations had names and the Fat Girl stood next to her car and tried to pick them out. Cathedral Rock. Castle Rock. Bell Rock. Coffeepot Rock. But their names weren't what was amazing. It was the red. It was deep and vibrant and, against the bright blue sky, it was somehow a wonderful wound in the earth's ceiling.

Every word for red came to the Fat Girl's mind as she stood there. Cardinal, burgundy, ruby, fuchsia, magenta, scarlet, vermillion. And they all fit. They all soared. The Fat Girl found herself wanting to stretch her fingers toward them, to see if the colors burned. She burned with pleasure and awe.

The red formations were also big and beautiful, just like the Grand Canyon was supposed to be. Standing there, the Fat Girl felt a kinship, a connection, that she'd never felt before. She thought of the number of times she'd seen women gushing over the held-out finger of a feminine hand. The glimmer of an engagement ring, a tiny rock so chiseled and polished, it resembled the fragment of a fallen star. And yes, diamonds were beautiful. But these rocks. They stopped traffic. People stood alone and in clusters, trying to own the rocks on their digital cameras. The Fat Girl knew, even as she held up her own camera, that it was the memory that would impress. It was impossible to represent the red rocks well on a digital screen. In her mind, they would stay large and soaring. And grounded. Impossibly attached to the earth as their limbs and fingers tore open the sky.

Grounded. The Fat Girl, for the first time ever, felt a part of the earth. Connected to it. Represented by it.

As she climbed into her car, she thought about changing her plans, about finding a hotel here and giving up on the Grand Canyon. How could it be any more incredible than this? But she remembered the shopgirl in the food court. "There's not even a word for it," she'd said. There were words for these rocks, they flooded the Fat Girl's brain with color and magnitude and majesty. The Fat Girl decided to go on ahead to the Grand Canyon, to be astonished into silence, and maybe stop again at Sedona during her second week. To replace the still unknown silence with these red words. The Grand Canyon was still an hour and a half away.

But the Fat Girl was reluctant to leave and so she quickly found a place for lunch, where she could sit outside at her leisure and look at the rocks while she ate. She called home, Large & Luscious, to say hello and let everyone know she arrived safely, but mostly, to tell them what she saw. The manager answered.

"I was just thinking about you," she said. "Where are you? Hang on, I'm going to put you on speaker phone so that everyone can hear."

The Fat Girl heard the click and then she called out a hello. "I'm having lunch," she said. "I'm in Sedona. It's… incredible. There are these red mountains, formations, rocks…I'm not sure what they are. But they're so beautiful." The word beautiful never felt so futile.

"I've seen pictures," the manager said. "I've always thought it would be a perfect place for a concert. A revival. Like Woodstock."

The Fat Girl thought about music rolling up and over the formations, climbing up Castle Rock, filling the Coffeepot, storming the Cathedral, and somehow, it seemed an affront. It seemed that the rocks should provide their own music, or that music would be inspired around them, from the trees and the moon and the whisper of grasses. "I've never seen anything like this," the Fat Girl said.

"When will you get to the Grand Canyon?" the manager asked.

"There's still a ways to go. I'll be there mid-afternoon," the Fat Girl said. She set down her sandwich and tried to collect her thoughts. "I wanted to tell you…I just wanted to tell you…"

"Tell us what?" said one of the Fat Girls.

"Spit it out!" said another, and laughed.

"Well, I wanted to tell you how I feel here. It's just so different." The Fat Girl fell silent and the women at Large & Luscious fell silent too, like they did during their in-store secret conversations. The Fat Girl couldn't even hear any customers, any clothes being shuffled along metal bars. "No customers?" she asked.

"It's quiet right now," the manager said. "What did you want to say?"

The Fat Girl looked again at the red rocks, the sun splashing down their sides, a warm fall of light and golden sparks. "It's just…well, you know what it's like to stand by Lake Michigan? How it feels so deep and wild sometimes, like it's alive, and you just stand there and look because it's so beautiful, but it's something else, it's a lake, it's not you. You're apart from it. You just admire it."

There was silence again and the Fat Girl wished she could see their faces. Then the manager said, "Yes, I know. Go on."

"The rocks…they're not different. It's like…it's like looking at us. Like looking at me. Or at least…that's how it feels. They're just so big. And they're just so beautiful."

The Fat Girl did hear something this time. A snort. It came from the table behind her, and when she looked over her shoulder, she saw a man who quickly began to study his plate. The Fat Girl turned back and closed her eyes. "I have to go," she whispered. "I need to get moving."

"Okay. Have fun. It sounds just lovely," the manager said. "Really. Just go, and then tell us what you see."

The Fat Girl folded her phone, then quickly cleaned up her table. She didn't look at the man behind her again. She didn't look at the red rocks. She hurried to her car.

The ride between Sedona and the Grand Canyon wound up through the mountains until the Fat Girl wondered if she was on the launchpad to Heaven. Then she went down a steep incline, twisted through a town, and suddenly, the land squashed flat. It was as if someone, maybe God, just got tired of building the mountains and quit. The road became straight and boring and the Fat Girl had to fight to stay awake.

As she approached the Grand Canyon, she began seeing signs, advertising hotels and restaurants and gift shops.

There was even a sign to visit a spiritual white buffalo. The Fat Girl wondered what it was about an animal being white that made it feel sacred. In Wisconsin, there were white deer and white squirrels and both were treated as talismans. She thought of the red rocks of Sedona and didn't think they would look any more sacred in white.

Then she was through the gates of the park, but even so, it seemed to take forever to get to Bright Angel. At one point, there was a large parking lot and people lined four-deep along a brick fence. The Fat Girl assumed they were looking at the canyon, and so she drove through the lot, craning her neck to see beyond the crowd. At one point, a family stepped away and the Fat Girl caught a glimpse and she involuntarily gasped. Just that little look made her shiver and she suddenly hunched over her wheel with anticipation.

Finally, she was at her cabin. It was definitely colder here and the Fat Girl could see her breath, glistening in the thin and dry air. She was glad she brought her jacket. Quickly, the Fat Girl dropped her suitcase and her book on the bed and she bundled up. Tucking the cabin keys in her pocket, she made her way out the door, past the other cabins, and followed a path marked with wooden arrows, pointing the way to the the Grand Canyon. She wondered, for a moment, how she couldn't sense it coming, since it was so big. Wasn't it everywhere?

And then it was. The Fat Girl reached a cliff and the vista opened up before her, taking up every inch of her sight and the horizon. Instead of soaring up, the Grand Canyon soared down, and down some more, seeming to expose the heart of the earth. The Fat Girl thought again of a wound, like the wound in the sky in Sedona, but here, the earth's chest was opened up and pulled back. It took her breath away, and her equilibrium too, and for a moment, she swayed. She reached out and grabbed a tree.

The reds were here as well, but trickled with oranges and browns, a lacy fleur-de-lis of minerals running through earthen sinews and veins. There was ledge after ledge after ledge and the Fat Girl could see people moving, miles down, as they worked their way to the bottom. The Fat Girl wondered how they would ever make it back up.

When she had her bearings again, the Fat Girl moved down the South Rim trail. There were no barricades, no rails, no fences, and the path was dry and dusty. The Fat Girl kept one hand on the wall of rock beside her, to maintain her steadiness, to keep from stepping over the edge. She didn't go far, knowing it would be difficult for her to climb back up, and eventually, she stopped and leaned against the wall, faced out and looked down. The world wavered again for a moment, but then her vision cleared.

And it was big. It was beautiful. And there were simply no words. The Fat Girl thought of the glazed shopgirl in the food court and the Fat Girl felt glazed too.

The Fat Girl stood there for a while longer, not moving, just looking, her hands pressed flat behind her on the wall, touching what she saw below. Becoming, she felt, a part of it. She could be a rock formation. She was an escarpment.

Then a family walked down, and the Fat Girl pressed further into the wall to let them pass. The father told the children to be careful as they stepped around the Fat Girl, and the mother muttered something about how some people weren't anything but unthinking dangerous obstacles on the path and if they couldn't handle the trail, they shouldn't be on it. After the family went around a corner, the Fat Girl took a deep breath, and made her way back up.

She stayed on the top of the rim for a while, walking along it, keeping her eyes over and out as much as possible. Never losing the connection. When the sun went down, even though it was behind the Fat Girl, it splashed color over the sky. The canyon, in response, seemed to darken. The Fat Girl watched as the sunset's colors shifted into a deep blue, sinking into profound black, and then she tore herself away. She returned to her cabin, retrieved her poetry book and her purse and walked to the restaurant for supper.

The Fat Girl's night was restless. She kept thinking about the canyon, just a short walk away, but sealed out of sight by the absolute darkness. In an odd sort of way, it felt like the canyon disappeared, and the Fat Girl was anxious for its return. In the connecting cabin next door, there was a couple who didn't seem to miss the canyon, didn't seem to mind the darkness, filling the hours with almost continuous love-making, punctuated with banging and moans and cries. The Fat Girl kept her mind focused on the canyon, away from something she didn't know and didn't know if she ever would. After a while, she turned on a light and opened her book and read poetry until she fell asleep.

Her alarm was set early, so that she could stumble out and watch the sun rise over the canyon. Though she hadn't slept much, the Fat Girl woke up eager. She dressed quickly and warmly and then decided to bring her book of poetry with her, in case she decided to head right up for breakfast, instead of going back to sleep.

The Fat Girl was one of the first to arrive. She moved carefully down the South Rim trail, until she found a place where she could stand steadily without having to lean against the wall, but the wall was there if she needed it. Soon she heard the shuffling feet of others, the muffled voices, whispers in the early morning. When someone said, "Excuse me," she moved forward even though she knew she was expected to move back. She was determined not to lose her spot, even if it meant standing nearer to the edge. She wanted to be as close to the canyon as possible, intimate herself as much as possible. She heard and felt someone slip in behind her.

Then it was almost like a curtain opened. The sky showed a ribbon of red, fluttered through with gold, and everyone fell silent. There were no sighs, no coughs, no exclamations. The Fat Girl stood, her poetry book clasped in front of her, and she watched.

An artist at work. A brush of orange here, a surprise of purple there. Gold shot throughout. The sun, slivered, semi-circled, half-circled, full-circled, over the horizon, and then there was a wash of orange and red and yellow to the canyon below. Sky reflected canyon, canyon refracted sky, they joined and blended. The sense of depth disappeared, became a living mass of hue, a pudding, a stew. The Fat Girl breathed and felt the light soak into her skin.

There was a scree and the Fat Girl looked up. Between the sun and the canyon, a hawk flew, its wingspan broad and delicate. The Fat Girl watched the soar and her mind connected with a poem from the night before. One of the words for red came to mind too.

Moving slowly, so as not to disturb the art, the breath, the sun, the sky, the canyon itself, the Fat Girl raised her book and opened it. She found Girard Manley Hopkins' "The Windhover," which even last night struck her more as an aubade than a poem. Strongly, she read it out loud in a clear voice. She didn't care who heard. She wanted the hawk to hear. She wanted the canyon to hear.

I caught this morning morning's minion, kingdom
of daylight's dauphin, dappled dawn-drawn Falcon, in his riding
Of the rolling level underneath him steady air, and striding
High there, how he rung upon the rein of a wimpling wing
In his ecstasy! then off, off forth on a swing,
As a skate's heel sweeps smooth on a bow-bend: the hurl and gliding
Rebuffed the big wind. My heart in hiding
Stirred for a bird,—the achieve of, the mastery of the thing!

Brute beauty and valor and act, oh, air, pride, plume, here
Buckle! And the fire that breaks from thee then, a billion
Times told lovelier, more dangerous, o my chevalier!

No wonder of it: sheer plod makes plough down sillion
Shine and blue-bleak embers, ah my dear,
Fall, gall themselves, and gash gold-vermillion.

The Fat Girl heard her voice ring out, sending the words into the air and to the canyon like the colors from the sunrise. Her words were a part of the canyon, her voice too, and she herself. Her feet melted into the rock, she felt her body become one with it, she made love to the canyon and the canyon made love to her, just like the couple in the cabin next door, but with the silence of dignity, the reverence of love and acceptance. For a moment, she closed her eyes, raised her arms out like the hawk's wings, and she drew in the canyon. The Fat Girl and the Grand Canyon were big. They were beautiful.

Then a woman behind her said, "If you're done with your reading, do you think you can move? We want a picture and you're blocking the sunrise."

The Fat Girl opened her eyes. The sunrise swept the earth, all the way from the left to the right. The sun was now fully above the canyon; the Fat Girl had to raise her chin to see it. Drawing her arms back around herself, she held the book to her chest and she shivered. But she felt her feet planted into the earth. Into the Grand Canyon. She belonged here.

Then a man's voice. "Hey, lady, c'mon. We asked you nicely. We want a picture of the sunrise before it's gone. Can you move your bulk please?" He moved forward, jostling her.

The Fat Girl looked at all the colors, brought wild by the sun. She thought of the Red Rocks of Sedona, the wound in the sky, and she looked at the canyon, the wound in the earth. The Fat Girl knew their hurt. They knew hers.

The man pushed again and the Fat Girl spread her wings, and the book tumbled, Gerard Manley Hopkins and Emily Dickinson taking flight. The Fat Girl fell into richness, strode high into big and beautiful. Then she galled herself gold vermillion.

BEING THE FAT GIRL'S MOTHER

The Fat Girl's mother never really thought of her daughter as fat until she turned twelve years old and got her period. When she began to bleed, she began to eat and she ate everything in sight. The Fat Girl's mother would come home from work and find her daughter sitting on the kitchen counter, her hand deep in a bag of potato chips, her mouth rimmed shiny with salt. Or she'd be sprawled on the couch in the den, watching endless television, and there'd be an empty package of Oreos beside her. A package that the Fat Girl's mother remembered buying just the day before.

The Fat Girl did indeed begin to round over. Her new breasts were round as cantaloupe, her tummy the oval round of a watermelon. In last year's bikini, she appeared to be ripening, bursting out of the tiny triangles of the top, sweetly curving out and over the bottom, her body delicious and ready to be sunk into with a hungry set of teeth. Or so the Fat Girl's mother thought, just for a second. Then she decided her daughter was fat.

It just wasn't easy being the Fat Girl's mother.

Years of diets ensued, trying to flush the bad food away, trying to shove the good food, in moderate portions, down the daughter's throat. First, Ayds candies, claiming to curb the appetite while making the mind think it was eating chocolate and caramel and mint instead of an appetite suppressant. The Fat Girl's mother thought sure this would work, until in a fit, the Fat Girl rebelled and ate an entire box of Ayds, then snuck out and bought a large Hershey bar and ate that too. The Fat Girl threw up for the next eight hours, and the Fat Girl's mother alternately rebuked her for being a glutton, and encouraged her with how much weight she would lose by vomiting.

Diet pills. They revved up the metabolism. Naturally, the ads said. The Fat Girl's mother doled out pills at breakfast and pills at dinner. She tried to sneak one in with the girl's home-packed salad, so the Fat Girl could have one at lunch, even though it wasn't allowed to send drugs of any kind, even natural, to school. But then she discovered that the Fat Girl was trading the pill for another girl's lunch. And the pills at home were slipped into a pocket, traded as well for other treats.

Grapefruit diet. Green bean diet. Water diet. Potions and panaceas and cures. And the Fat Girl managed to thwart them all. She swore she wanted to lose weight, swore she knew it was good for her, that she would look better, that, as she got older, the boys would call her for dates and for proms and for marriage. She promised and she promised and she ate. The Fat Girl's mother knew, from reading a diary, that food made the Fat Girl feel good right now. It was hard to think about feeling good in the future when you could feel good right now. The Fat Girl cried, sometimes, in her mother's presence. And she cried, sometimes, in her own room alone. And in the restroom at school. Or so the diary said. Who knew, really. Adolescent girls were dramatic.

It just wasn't easy being the Fat Girl's mother. She did her best to control the food that came into the house. But then the Fat Girl went to friends' houses after school, and who knew what she got there. So the Fat Girl's mother insisted that her daughter come home after school, she wasn't allowed to go to friends', and then the friends came over there and brought snacks with them. Which led to the Fat Girl's mother saying no to friends, and the Fat Girl had to call as soon as she got home to prove that she was there and nowhere else. The Fat Girl did, then went out again and made sure she was back in her room, not the kitchen, by the time the Fat Girl's mother got home. And what could the Fat Girl's mother do? She couldn't chain her to the bed, now, could she?

Well, she could, and she did, sneaking away from her job for a trip home and then back, but the Fat Girl's father found out and he roared. He said the Fat Girl could tell and the authorities could come and then where would they be, and so the Fat Girl's mother couldn't do that anymore.

It just wasn't easy. Being the Fat Girl's mother.

She tried a different tactic. She tried to camouflage the Fat Girl, she tried to hide the fatness. She bought her daughter clothes that were at least a size too big, so that people would think her daughter was really thin, but hiding it under an excess of material. But then the Fat Girl asked for money from her father. She went out with her friends to the mall and she bought clothes that fit, that were sometimes a size too small, and her curves billowed out like the sails of a great ship. The Fat Girl's mother tried to make sure the Fat Girl never wore those clothes, she shoved them in the back of the Fat Girl's closet, and she made sure that when the Fat Girl left for school in the morning, she was in big jeans and a big shirt. But then the Fat Girl changed clothes at school, into an outfit dug out and tucked away in her backpack. So the Fat Girl's mother searched her backpack, chucking out clothes and contraband food.

Then the Fat Girl's friends smuggled the clothes in for her and the Fat Girl just kept them in her locker. The Fat Girl's mother heard about it from a friend, who happened to mention that her daughter and the Fat Girl wore the exact same outfit one day, and weren't they cute, and the Fat Girl's mother knew that she never purchased the outfit described. At the end of the school day, the Fat Girl's mother met the Fat Girl at her locker. She emptied it of all the too-tight clothes, the food, all of it, right there in front of the Fat Girl and her friends and her enemies and her teachers. The Fat Girl wailed, banging her head against the locker next door. A counselor tried to intervene, but the Fat Girl's mother quickly got in between and herded her daughter out the door. She drove the Fat Girl home and she stripped her and she took the clothes and the food to the back yard, threw them into a pile, and lit a match. A huge bonfire. While the clothes burned, the Fat Girl pressed herself, naked, against her bedroom window, and she screamed. But the Fat Girl's bedroom was in the front of the house, not the back, and so anyone passing by could see the glass-squashed breasts, the tummy, a few good curls of pubic hair. And the wide-open mouth.

And that's how the Fat Girl's father found her when he pulled his car into the driveway. He ran into the house and then out through the back because he smelled smoke and he found the Fat Girl's mother tending the pyre. He backhanded her, nearly putting her into the flames, and he told her the whole neighborhood could smell the smoke and know it wasn't leaves, and the whole neighborhood could hear the Fat Girl's screams and see her naked body against the bedroom window. He said the authorities could be called and then where would they be. Leaving his wife weeping on her back by the flames, he went inside and pulled the Fat Girl by her hair away from the window and tossed her onto her bed. There, for the first time, he plainly saw the new curves and the swirls of pubic hair. She was lying on the bed and his wife was still flat out by the fire and there was no one else to see. If no one could see, then there was no place else to be. There would be no authorities. He would make sure. He closed and locked the door.

The Fat Girl's mother finally came in, after picking herself up and dousing the fire with the hose, soaking every single one of the embers, keeping the ashes from even floating in the air because she didn't want anyone to see her daughter's ashes floating into their yards. She checked in the powder room mirror and put an icepack on her eye. The Fat Girl's father was in the shower. She asked him what he wanted for dinner and he said chicken. The Fat Girl was in her shower too, which made the Fat Girl's mother angry; two showers at once wasted hot water. When the Fat Girl's mother told her to get out of the shower and come down and set the table, the Fat Girl said she wasn't hungry and she wouldn't be eating dinner that night. The Fat Girl's mother went downstairs to set the table herself, and she thought maybe her tactics had worked, although it had gotten her backhanded on the lawn.

It just wasn't easy being the Fat Girl's mother.

It was quiet for a patch, with the Fat Girl silent and sullen, but not eating, at home anyway, so that was a good thing. But then on a Sunday, the Fat Girl took off to the mall with her friends and when she came home, her big shirt was spattered with ketchup and mustard and ice cream and cheese and some things that just weren't identifiable. She held her head down and went right past her mother and up to her bedroom. A friend who came to the door said the Fat Girl had a fit of sorts, went to every restaurant in the food court and ate at every single one and didn't even swallow before the next forkful went in. The friend said she and the other girls just didn't know what to do when the Fat Girl spread the food on a table and threw the fork away and just plowed her face in. They waited until she was finished, cleaned her up some, dried her tears, and then brought her home.

The Fat Girl's mother went upstairs and found her daughter sprawled on her back on her bed. She scolded the Fat Girl, asking her what she was thinking, what she was doing, how she could make such a spectacle of herself. The

Fat Girl didn't say anything, she just stared up at the ceiling. She stared without blinking. The Fat Girl's mother pulled her daughter to her feet and set her in front of the full-length mirror behind the bedroom door. She yanked the shirt over her daughter's head, unbuckled her bra, slid her pants and her undies down to the floor. "Look at yourself," she said. "Just look at yourself. Don't you see how disgusting you are? You are fat, you are fat, you are fat!" She pushed her daughter, tripping over her ankle-bound pants, and when they reached her shower, she shoved her in. "Clean yourself, you smell like a pig and you have mustard in your hair," she said, and then the Fat Girl's mother went downstairs. The shower, she noticed, went on for a long time.

 The Fat Girl didn't come down to dinner. She went straight to bed.

 When the Fat Girl's mother went upstairs that night, turning out the lights along the way, she looked in on her daughter, who seemed to be sleeping, and she looked in the bathroom, where jeans, panties, socks and shoes were sodden on the shower floor. The Fat Girl's mother sighed and put the things in the hamper, the shoes in the trash. Then she went to bed and stared at the ceiling too, just like her daughter a few hours before. She thought about taking a shower herself. Then she told the Fat Girl's father about what happened at the mall. She said all the girls watched their daughter make a pig of herself, transform a mall table into a trough and she threw herself into it. She said they all saw, the friends, the strangers, the mall workers, maybe even the security guards, who knew? Who knew who all saw, who knew who could call, and where would they be if someone did? She said she wondered about sending the Fat Girl to a Fat Farm. She told her husband that it just wasn't easy being the Fat Girl's mother.

 He got out of bed and said it was time for him to take care of this. She told him the girl was asleep, she was quiet in her bed, but he just glared over his shoulder, then walked

Enlarged Hearts

down the hall. The Fat Girl's mother heard the door close, then lock, and for a while, it was silent. She wondered what he was doing, if he was just standing there, staring at the flesh mountain, the overripe fruit salad, that used to be their little girl. But then she heard the Fat Girl's cries and the squeaking of the bed and it was a sound she heard before. She'd made it herself, when she sat on that bed and spanked the Fat Girl's bare bottom. She remembered spanking and spanking and spanking and the little girl crying. Even then, her bottom was round. But the Fat Girl's mother stopped when the Fat Girl began to bleed. She stopped when the Fat Girl was twelve. She wondered if the Fat Girl wasn't too old for spankings now, for spankings on a bare round behind. But still, it was something the Fat Girl's mother hadn't tried, hadn't resurrected, and maybe the Fat Girl's father's authority was just the thing that would do the trick. After all, it worked on her, it worked on the Fat Girl's mother. Her heart thickened with hope. When the Fat Girl's father came back to bed, the Fat Girl's mother asked if everything was okay now. He grunted and rolled away.

With the rising of the sun came the rising of doubts. After the Fat Girl's mother kissed her husband goodbye and sent her silent daughter out the door in too-big clothes, she sat down and called all her friends who had friends who went to Fat Farms. She did her research. She made the calls, talked the talk, brought out the unused credit card. Fourteen days later, when school was out, the Fat Girl went off to a Fat Farm in South Carolina for six weeks.

Six weeks without the Fat Girl. The Fat Girl's mother felt her mood lighten. She kept the girl's room neat and clean, sunlight pouring in through opened windows. She found a beautiful glass nightlight, with colors like a sunrise, and for six weeks, the room was never dark. She made nice dinners for herself and her husband, meals where she didn't have to worry, and they ate and drank wine and listened to music. They went to movies. And at night, for the first time in a long time, the Fat Girl's father didn't roll away. The Fat Girl's mother opened her legs and remembered the joy of life before child. Before the blood came and before the battle began and before her life was taken over by poundage. She felt the firmness of her husband's hand, but not the fist, and she held him against herself, and she rejoiced in the body she still had, the body that became so ignored when the Fat Girl became fat.

It just wasn't easy being the Fat Girl's mother.

On the day her daughter came home, the Fat Girl's mother wasn't happy. Even if her daughter was thin, she would still be there, and maybe the gloom would return. With the gloom would be the tension and with the tension would be the fist and the rolling away in bed, the squeak and the cry from the other room.

But then the Fat Girl walked down the aisle of the airport toward her mother. She walked toward her on long legs, her gaze level, her hair loose and rolling over her shoulders. The Fat Girl's mother melted. There was a beautiful girl. There was the child she gave birth to, the one she knew would do great things, would be breathtaking, would be able to have any man she wanted, would have long golden curls and a slender body and a walk that would draw everyone's attention. There she was. The Fat Girl's mother exclaimed. The Fat Girl wore size two jeans, a spaghetti strap top that left her belly bare, and white high-heeled sandals. She was tanned. But she didn't smile. When the Fat Girl's mother hugged her, she was stiff.

The Fat Girl's father smiled at the Fat Girl that night, greeting his daughter at dinner. He hugged her close and his arms overlapped around her. And for a while, all was well. But it didn't take long. And then it started again. The eating, the sneaking, the pigs into troughs. The sighing, the staring, the rolling away. The pounds. The pounds. The pounds.

It wasn't easy, being the Fat Girl's mother.

Years later, when the Fat Girl married, she wore a size 20 wedding gown. It was a gown that was special-ordered through the Large & Luscious Large Women's Clothing Boutique in the mall. The Fat Girl's mother was too mortified to go inside with the Fat Girl on the day the dress arrived. The Fat Girl went in alone and disappeared into the dressing rooms, followed by two enormous clerks. The Fat Girl's mother sat across the mall aisle, on a bench facing the Petite Sophisticate.

No matter what the Fat Girl's mother did, she couldn't make her daughter look beautiful on her special day. No matter what, there were still yards upon yards upon yards of white silk. White lace. White tulle. An abundance. An over-abundance. There was just too much.

The Fat Girl was marrying an older man, twenty years her senior. It was, the Fat Girl's mother supposed, the best she could hope for. He'd been married before, divorced two times, and both previous wives were out of state and out of communication. No children. And he looked, the Fat Girl's mother thought, like a side of ham. His hands were always folded into briskets.

After the Fat Girl's father walked the Fat Girl up the aisle, he lifted the veil from her face. And then he kissed her full on the lips. In front of everyone. Everyone could see. And the Fat Girl didn't step away. She kept her eyes closed, her bouquet held tightly at her side. When the Fat Girl's father moved into his pew, he was crying. The Fat Girl's mother carefully, so that no one could see, edged away from her husband. If someone would see, then where would they be? She moved herself further away.

The Fat Girl looked over at her then, looked over at her mother, dipping her chin on her right shoulder. Her golden curls fell to where her waist was implied. She was all in white. She was in a size 20. She didn't smile. She didn't cry. She looked away. She put her hand into her husband's brisket fist.

The Fat Girl's mother knew, she just knew, her daughter was going to have a miserable life.

It just wasn't easy, being the Fat Girl's mother.

THE FAT GIRL TAKES THE LONG WAY

The Fat Girl actually tried a lot of times, even before she was fat. She started when she was the Goth Girl, dressed all in black, her hair dyed to match and spiky like a pincushion, eyes charcoaled and lined, lips like night. She was underweight then, and she tried suicide for the first time when she was fifteen, and again at sixteen, twice at seventeen, and reworked her plan at eighteen. She just didn't do well at suicide, obviously, always chickening out and botching up at the last minute. The slashes in the wrists horizontal instead of vertical, the pills swallowed, but only half the bottle before she began retching, the car directed toward a tree, but screamed sideways and the passenger door got smashed instead. Walking into Lake Michigan late at night under a full moon, striding until the water closed over her head, opening her mouth and breathing darkness in, passing out…and then washing up on shore, freezing cold, missing a sneaker and a sock, with seaweed stuck to her hair like green extensions.

The Fat Girl went away to college and followed that lifestyle of late breakfasts and early drinks, junk food lunches, dinners of more, and middle-of-the-night pizza delivery. Coming back home at Thanksgiving with the freshman fifteen and her backpack saddled to her body, she told her older sister what she'd been eating. "That stuff'll kill you," her sister said, her sister with the nurse's degree, her sister who'd eaten her way through two pregnancies so far and Jenny Craiged herself back down to pre-baby weight. The Fat Girl digested the information and then changed her ways.

She switched to jeans with an elastic waistband, loose flowing shirts with draped sleeves. She stopped dying her hair, letting it return to its normal brown, and as it grew, she parted it down the middle. And she ate. The clothes skimmed, then strained over her developing curves, and her hair soon fell down her shoulders, her breasts peekabooing out through a split cascade of waves. Her face was clean.

From blooming, she traveled on to bursting. From bursting to burgeoning, and then to beyond. The Fat Girl was eating to kill.

Herself.

It was a slow process and though she tried to vocalize her reasons, she never seemed to find the right words. Or she said the right words, but no one around her seemed to understand their significance. "Why are you sad all the time?" her parents asked. "We give you so much." And the Fat Girl agreed, through years spent in a room filled with toys, then electronics, then clothes, then moving to an expensive private dorm, and finally to her own apartment, where her parents gifted her with the security deposit and first month's rent and the furniture from her childhood room and a new sofa and kitchen set besides. But "I still feel empty," she said, and she did, even standing in the apartment that was her home, surrounded by the familiar and new. "Why are you so depressed all the time?" her sister asked, offering to provide her with information on all the latest antidepressants and diet pills. "Because all the happiness around me only seems to swirl in the air," the Fat Girl said. "I'm aware of it, but none of it settles on me. It's like watching a movie screen, filled with pink and orange and yellow smiley faces. I can see it. But I'm not in it." The Fat Girl's sister shook her head and brought home more samples.

After college, when the Fat Girl got a job at the Large & Luscious Large Women's Clothing Boutique in the mall, the manager said, "You need to at least smile at the customers, please," and the sales staff nodded and bared their teeth. The Fat Girl bared hers too, but when she took advantage of her discount, she reverted back to Goth black, diluted it with some white, and she kept her make-up neutral.

Though sometimes at work, when she wasn't thinking, when she was caught off guard, when she was swept into the giddiness of all girls in a group, the hormones and camaraderie bubbling to the top, the Fat Girl laughed. And sometimes at night, when she lay in bed and her thoughts rolled like a ticker tape, recalling the events and conversations of the day, the Fat Girl laughed again, the sound foreign in the lights-out of her apartment. At those moments, the Fat Girl felt alien to herself, strange and oddly buoyant, like an inflatable floatie in a pool.

But still, the pounds came on. Every six months or so, slower as she got older, the Fat Girl donated her wardrobe to Goodwill and restocked her closet with black and white clothes in the next size up. She tried to choose the same shirts, the same pants, to keep the girls at work and her family from realizing just how quickly she was growing. And she threw in a new outfit every now and then too, just to keep them guessing. It got to the point where the Fat Girl didn't even try things, she just picked out the next size, paid for them and put them on. If her sister or her mother ever said anything about her outfits, like "Nice pattern," or "That looks good on you," rare but good-hearted compliments, the Fat Girl just shrugged and said, "Oh, thanks, but I've worn this before."

Through it all, the Fat Girl went to the doctor religiously, keeping track of her journey. Her blood pressure climbed and she faithfully filled the prescriptions, but didn't swallow the pills. Her breathing became ragged and she accepted inhalers for "exercise-induced asthma," of all things; the only exercise she got was heaving her body around. She stuck those inhalers in a box under her bed. Her joints ached, her back ached, her knees threatened to give out, and the Fat Girl nodded over the directions on how to take anti-inflammatories and pain medications, and then she stored those too. Acid reflux meds, to put out the fire in her throat and her gut, but the Fat Girl felt the burn as a harbinger of the death she'd always wanted. At one point, her doctor even gave her an anti-depressant, one that her sister never mentioned, a new supersonic psychotropic, guaranteed to bring glee and glory in one little pill, just in case, the doctor said, depression was the root of her problem. Which made the Fat Girl laugh. She did take those for a week, just to see, just to experiment with drug-induced joy, but no supersonic miracle happened; happiness still refused to come off the screen and settle into her bloodstream. She looked at herself in the mirror and wondered how she could still feel so empty, as full as she was, but she did, and that's all there was to it.

The Fat Girl was a pharmacy of unused medication. The bathroom cabinet was full, and several plastic tubs were overflowing beneath her bed. The shelves in her closets were lined with pill bottles too, and she knew she would soon run out of space. She never threw the meds away…if she ever changed her mind and decided to go faster rather than slower, if she ever decided to see if adulthood brought with it a greater ability to do herself in, she wanted to be ready.

Now fifty-three, the Fat Girl was pretty much alone. Her parents had died, the Fat Girl donning the same black dress in two different sizes for each of their funerals. Her sister, who eventually birthed five children, was now the grandmother of ten, and she'd moved to another state and delighted in doubling her maternity. There were only the girls at Large & Luscious, and the Fat Girl still bared her teeth with them, even though her teeth were falling apart, in the hopes that a dental infection would spread from her mouth to her brain or to her heart.

While she still found herself engulfed in giggles from time to time, the Fat Girl, for the most part, was a large black boulder, rolling through the racks of oversized clothes, her own body just one size away from the largest they offered. Most of the sales staff hovered in the twenties, wearing clothing that was size 22, 24, 26. A few made it to thirty. But only the Fat Girl and one now dead other, among all the employees, had ever made it to 48. She wondered when she would hit that fifty mark, the big five-oh, the final size in the store. Everything after that had to be special-ordered and shipped as women that size tended to be bed-ridden.

When an especially large woman rumbled into the store, a woman who required the hidden double-wide mirror, all of the other clerks stepped back and let the Fat Girl take over. Her size gave her a special talent; the ability to understand what it was like to wear clothes that were more drapery than fashion, clothes that were wider than they were long, clothes that made a half-assed effort to look hip, using the same material as the rest of the styles in the store, but no zippers, no buttons, no snaps, no waistlines, no bustlines, nothing. Just elastic on the waistband of the pants and then yards and yards of fabric. The Fat Girl knew that with these women, silence was best, just smiles and pointing and nods, stuck in between the heaving breaths of a body overtaxed just by movement. She led them back to the special dressing room, twice the generous size of the others, and then, if the customer wanted, she led them back to the quickly and surreptitiously set up double mirror, created because mirrors of this size could never fit in a single dressing room, even the special dressing room. She stood behind these large women, twitching and futzing with the fabric, pampering and patting shoulders, as if attending to a model. She accepted their money too, folding their clothes gently into pink shopping bags and sending them on their way without a word between them, other than Thank you, from both customer and Fat Girl, at the end.

The Fat Girl had assumed years ago that she would turn fifty and hit size 50 at the same time, which seemed fitting, and even poetic, but it didn't turn out that way. At fifty, she wore size 42, and it took three years to get to 48, and now, the clothes were finally tightening again. To the Fat Girl, size 50 was It, the moment of reckoning, the moment her body would bend to her will and take itself out of this world and into another. A world she refused to imagine, but secretly believed would be better, would be a place where she could be sad and accepted. A place where feeling empty was normal, where depression was simply a state of mind, a lifestyle, and not a disease, so that the depressed wouldn't feel a need to hide. And if there was no need to hide, then maybe happiness would find her.

Because, the Fat Girl reasoned, if all the black-clad and empty people of the world came together in one place, maybe their emptinesses would spill into each other's and then they wouldn't be so empty anymore. It would be like Molokai, where leprosy wasn't even noticed because everyone was a leper. Heaven as a leper colony, a black and bleak depression colony. Heaven as Molokai. Once, the Fat Girl made herself laugh out loud in the middle of the night when she thought how Leper Colony and Leaper Colony weren't so very far apart. Then she changed Molokai to Mellowkai, to Morosekai and Mentalkai, and she laughed all over again. But even as she laughed, the thought made the Fat Girl sad, and so she descended, as always, into a black sleep. She had to sleep on her back now, because she just couldn't roll on her sides anymore. If she tried, she fell out of the single bed she'd slept in all her life, scaring the people in the apartment below.

For weeks, the Fat Girl courted the size 50. One morning, she would wake up, and her pants would be just a hair short of totally constricting her breathing. Then the next morning, she would swear out loud when a different pair of pants, same size, felt looser, and not yet terribly uncomfortable. It was like the size 50 was courting her too, playing a hard-to-get game with the conclusion of her life, the marriage of the Fat Girl to What She Wanted And Couldn't Quite Accomplish.

The Fat Girl started adding fifteen minutes extra to her lunchbreaks, piling more food on her tray, and at her coffee break in the morning and in the afternoon, she asked for a double helping of whipped cream in her whole milk cappuccinos.

And then finally came the day, or the work-week, actually, five days in a row, Monday through Friday, because her seniority guaranteed that she never had to work weekends. Five days in a row, all five pairs of her pants, in black, gray, and navy blue, dug into her flesh. The shirts pulled at her underarms and rode up over her stomach.

This was It.

On Friday, the Fat Girl volunteered to close, shooing the others gently out the door, telling them she didn't have plans anyway, she never had plans, did she? The other Fat Girls smiled and laughed, standing on the other side of the glass sliding doors, waving goodbye, until the Fat Girl clicked the lock and dimmed the lights. Only one light created a white gold aura over the cash register so that the Fat Girl could balance everything out and prepare the deposit.

But before she did, she slipped quietly through the racks of clothes, determining which size 50 outfit she would buy. She only needed one, she reasoned. She would only have the chance to wear it once.

She moved through the blacks and blacks-and-whites, and then, suddenly giddy, turned to the colors. Maybe she should go out with a splash. Maybe she would go brightly to the other side, dressed for the happiness that would come when she was accepted as she was, when she could reflect out what was sent her way, instead of always having to deflect jovial attempts to cheer her up.

In the denim rack, she found a size 50 jeans skirt, voluminous, with colorful stitching on the back pockets and down the seams on each side. Paging through the shirts, she found a red and white floral number that somehow reminded her of the sixties and hippies and the freedom that era carried with it. Belled sleeves, whooshy fabric, a fake belt stitched to create the sense of separation between her breasts and her stomach. Over in the shoe section, in the post-season clearance, there was a bright red pair of flip-flops, and the Fat Girl decided that for the first time in well over twenty years, she would let her feet bare themselves in public. She also picked out new panties, but she turned away from the bras, choosing instead to let her breasts remain loose and rolling after she released them for the final time from underwires and straps and quadruple rows of hooks.

Against her routine, the Fat Girl took all the new clothes into the special fitting room and she stripped. She left her old clothes neatly folded in a pile, topping it with her white and tattered underwire bra, a snow-capped peak to a fabric mountain. Then she pulled on her new things, marveling at how the skirt left her legs remarkably free to move. She snuggled the fake belt under her breasts and she almost laughed at the way her nipples suddenly popped out at the new sensation of nonsupportive fabric right against them. She wiggled her toes in the flip-flops. She didn't even look in the mirror, knowing she would never be able to appear fully in it, and she didn't care. She went by how she felt, rather than how she looked. Whether it was the new size, or the flow of the fabric, or the bright of the colors, the Fat Girl felt lighter. No, she didn't feel lighter, she felt light. She was almost floating.

After calculating her discount and paying for her clothes, the Fat Girl settled the store into security light safeness, collected the deposit bag, and stepped out into the mall, making sure the glass doors were locked behind her, the alarm set. Her flip-flops, away from the carpet and now on the linoleum of the hall, cheerfully smack-smacked as she headed for the parking lot.

She knew exactly where to go. She knew exactly where it would happen. The place was selected years ago, really, on the night of her last suicide attempt when she was seventeen years old. There was a spot on Lake Michigan that she loved, a little cove of sorts between two bluffs, where the sand was soft and usually free of bird droppings and dead fish. At night, and in early December, she knew she'd probably be alone. It was after ten. There wasn't a full moon, like last time, but a quarter, a sideways smile from the sky. Or, she supposed, it could be a sad downturned mouth, depending on which way she tilted her head and looked at it. Maybe, she thought, this is what the Leaper Colony would be like. Smile, frown, smile, frown, interchangeable. The same thing.

The Fat Girl hadn't been here in years. There was a long rotted wooden stairway leading down to the cove, and on her last visit, in her early forties, she believed, she no longer trusted her weight on the steps. Now, she figured if she fell, it didn't much matter. She was on her way out anyway. Even so, she held on to the banister where it looked stable, and overhanging tree branches where it didn't. And in a few places, she double-stepped, avoiding some particularly rotten wood. She laughed at herself for her caution, and her flip-flops laughed with her.

Finally on the beach, about twenty feet from the water, the scene stretched out, as beautiful as a softly lit painting in a darkened library. It was beautiful when she was seventeen, and it was beautiful now. Amazing how some things stayed the same. The rhythm of the waves, similar, she was told, to the sound of the ocean, was always a balm, and she remembered, from her early teen years, how she used to name them. This wave was Frank, that one Emily. This one Bob, that one Julia. And all of them kept rolling in to her, soaking her toes when she made it to the water, and surrounded her with never-ending company. Company that touched her and rolled back, touched her and rolled back, and never once asked her, "Why are you this way?"

The Fat Girl kicked off her new red flip-flops and then carefully lowered herself to the sand. It had been forever since she sat anywhere except on a couch, a chair, or a bed, and she worried for a moment about the possibility of getting herself back up. But then she remembered, chided herself, and settled down to wait. It was a quiet night except for the waves, and both the air and water were frosty, but the Fat Girl was almost always overheated and she welcomed the chill. This was the perfect place. She closed her eyes and waited for her body to let her go.

Which it didn't. The Fat Girl must have fallen asleep there, sitting, her chin lowered, her body like a massive egg, bottom-heavy into the ground. When she woke, her limbs felt stiff and solid, and at first, she couldn't move at all. She felt a coating on her skin, and when she opened her eyes, she saw that she sparkled, her body and hair agleam with tiny diamonds, her new clothes transformed to sparkling and angelic white. When her neck crackled and she could raise her head, she looked into a sunburst of reds and oranges and yellows, with the faint and delicate lines of silver filigree weaving in and out and up and down. The sound of her friends, the waves, was still there, low and quiet, steady as a heartbeat, and they were glittering too, through the gauze of Heaven. For a moment, she barely breathed, and she thought, oh, how lovely.

But then, she blinked, and the angel dust upon her face shattered and sprinkled like salt down to her chest.

She realized it had snowed.

And she recognized the great lake and the just-rising sun. She felt the sand beneath her. Around her, the ground was crusted with white. Her flip-flops had floated away. Through the translucence of the snow, her skin glowed blue on her exposed feet and hands.

She was still here. Her heart was thudding, slowly, she thought, but still here. With a shriek, she thrust her hands up so forcefully that she fell over onto her back and then she lay there, a bright lakeside snowdrift, speckled with red and blue.

The Fat Girl didn't really feel the cold. She was still sleepy, fatigue pulling at her as if she'd taken every one of the meds hoarded away in her apartment. Every one. As she closed her eyes again, she wondered how she was ever going to get up.

THE FAT GIRL GIVES GOOD CUSHION

It wasn't the move, it was the nature of the move, the Fat Girl thought as she swayed across the bar on a Friday night. At near closing time, the size of the body no longer mattered. All that mattered was the move itself. And the Fat Girl's move, hips on a roll, shoulders back, breasts heavy but lifted, gave out all the information these men needed to know. She would not be alone that night.

The Fat Girl was only fifteen years old the first time she heard the phrase, "More cushion, less pushin'." She heard it from the seventeen-year old boy flat on top of her in the woods behind their high school. When she gave in to him, when she decided it was time to surrender her virginity, he gasped on top of her and collapsed. She looked up at him and said, "But why did you want me?" And he, trying to collect his breath, said, "Oh, baby, more cushion, less pushin'. Damn, that was good!"

The Fat Girl didn't understand that phrase at first, but she took it as a compliment, and then went on to discover that it was apparently true. As soon as word got out that the Fat Girl was willing to cushion a boy, her size no longer mattered. She was invited to the back seats of cars during lunch breaks. She was invited to parties. She was invited to houses after school, to bedrooms and basement dens. She was even invited to school dances, though only in a group, and often several boys would slip away from their dates and meet her in the gym's locker room. Her cushion provided them with protection against the wall, against the floor, from themselves, and while she was the one who sometimes turned up bruised, she didn't care. The Fat Girl couldn't walk down the hall at school without some boy slinging his arm over her shoulder and drawing her into a nook somewhere. Even though she never made prom or homecoming queen, the Fat Girl knew she was easily as popular as the girls who did.

And now, as an adult, the Fat Girl still could have her fill of men. Pick a bar, pick a night, and walk in a certain way, and she was bound not to be lonely. It was the nature of the move.

When she went to work on Monday mornings, the Fat Girl always wore her softest pants, to comfort whatever level of chafing she'd received over the weekend. Still, her co-workers claimed to be able to tell how successful she'd been by the nature of her walk. The nature of the move, the nature of the walk; she swayed with sensuality one night, walked the careful step of used goods the next.

The Fat Girl worked in the mall, at the Large & Luscious Large Women's Clothing Boutique, a specialty shop for large women. The other girls who worked there looked at the Fat Girl with jealousy sometimes; so many of them just didn't have the confidence to follow nature and make moves for themselves. A few were in relationships, mostly lesbian, and a couple were married, but as far as the Fat Girl could tell, she was the only one who had sex on a regular basis, who could have it whenever she wanted it. "The nature of the move," she would tell them and slink across the floor to rearrange the silky huge lingerie. "More cushion, less pushin'," she'd crow and they'd all fall into waves of unsure laughter.

Most of the time anyway. Sometimes, when the Fat Girl came in with a particularly slow walk or with black bags under her eyes, some of the girls would demand, "How many of these men have you seen twice? Aren't you really still alone?"

The Fat Girl never answered. On those days, she volunteered to work in the back, behind the dressing rooms, checking on inventory, counting out pink Large & Luscious shopping bags. Because she hadn't seen any man twice. She took these men for a ride, gave them the best of everything she had, taking advantage of all her curves, her grooves, her cushion, and sometimes, they fell asleep with their heads nestled between her breasts. In the morning, she got up, scrounged around their pathetic kitchens, found enough food to make a decent breakfast, or if the situation was desperate, slipped out quickly to a corner bakery or restaurant, and then regaled the men with breakfast in bed. They always had her for breakfast too, and she would serve them, allowing them to turn her this way and that, offering up a breast, a hand, a mouth, until they rested upon her, panting, and echoed that seventeen-year old boy, with, "Damn, that was good!" Then a shower, and a long delicious kiss at the door…followed by no phone call. No email. No nothing. The Fat Girl learned to shrug it off, to go out the next night to a different bar. On those Mondays when the Fat Girl hid away in the back room, she always came out by lunchtime, saying to her co-workers, "The right one just hasn't come along yet. In the meantime…I'm getting my fill."

Until now. Now, even though the Fat Girl was getting her fill still, she was hungrier than ever. Because now, there was one man. A man she saw every Friday night, meeting him at the same bar downtown, drinking with him, rolling with him all night long. His name was Mark. Her Monday morning walk was no longer quite so painful, because she only saw him on Friday nights. He worked on Saturday nights. And after Mark on a Friday, she had no desire to nab another. She still went to the bar on Saturdays, but the nature of her move was different when she crossed the floor. She was smoother, she waltzed, her steps and eyes dreamy…men at the bar knew not to go after a woman in love. Contentment and satisfaction rode on her hips and when she sat at the bar on Saturday nights, she sat alone, but cloaked in the glow of the taken.

The Fat Girl was in love. She knew it. She knew it from the way she stared blankly over her armfuls of fitting room rejects every day, frozen even in the mindless act of shopbacking. She knew it because on one Saturday morning, as she left Mark's apartment, she filched one of his shirts from the laundry hamper in his bathroom, so she would have something with his scent at her own home. And she knew it because of the nature of her move, the way her hips felt unlocked when she walked, her arms loose and ready, her whole body on a roll toward marriage, toward children, toward waking up in the morning in a tangle of limbs that quickly became tangled with a purpose.

Making love with Mark, she felt her body open, felt herself open, in a way that never happened before. Dropping her knees further apart, she moaned as he slid further in, and she climbed into orgasm like a life preserver. When she cried out, she gripped his hips with her hands, clenched her thighs around him, and collected his entire body into her spasms. She held him there, clasped to herself, and when she opened her eyes, he was looking down at her.

"You okay?" he asked.

The Fat Girl smiled and answered in the way she'd heard since she was fifteen: "Damn, that was good!" He resumed his rhythm and she gave him his ride, joyous beneath him.

At work, the Fat Girl took her breaks in front of the store's computer terminal, looking at the online store which carried wedding dresses. The other girls teased her, but the Fat Girl only smiled, picturing herself in each voluminous dress, wondering if she should try to lose a little weight first, but then shaking it off. It was the nature of the move, after all, and it was her move at her size that drew him in.

One night, an echo burbled out of her throat in the afterglow and she looked up at him and said, "But why do you want me?"

In answer, he sucked on her throat and then nuzzled into her, sinking into her flesh the way a dog burrows into his bed. And she transformed herself around him, cushioning him, enveloping him and holding him tight.

At work, the Fat Girl went down one of the side aisles of the mall and into the travel agency. She picked up any brochure that showed white beaches, blue skies, sun and heat and skin. She and Mark would honeymoon at one of these places, they would soak in the warmth and plaster their bodies together. They would sit in their swimsuits on the beach, facing the seamless blue that was paradise water and sky, and the Fat Girl would be like any other woman there…loved. It was the nature of the move.

The Fat Girl tucked the brochures into her purse, to carry with her on Friday nights. She printed the pictures of the wedding dresses and tucked those in there too. The girls at Large & Luscious continued to tease her, but gently. The Fat Girl just smiled and moved through Friday nights and mid-week phone calls.

Waking in the early morning on a Saturday, the Fat Girl kissed Mark's shoulder and then made her way to the kitchen. She knew where everything was. She felt comfortable moving naked around his entire apartment, not worried about his catching her bending over or squatting or scratching her armpit. No matter where she was, no matter what she was doing, he would find her, run his hands over his favorite parts of her body, her breasts, her ass, the creased insides of her thighs, and he would encourage her into a kiss or an embrace or up against a wall or over a table. It was comfortable. She was comfortable.

Quietly, the Fat Girl prepared Mark's favorite breakfast. She knew his favorite breakfast, all the way down to how many mushrooms he liked in his omelet (he liked them fresh, halved, and about a dozen, please) and what kind of cheese (Monterey Colby Jack). She toasted his sourdough bread, buttered it, topped it with mixed fruit jelly. She made his coffee in the French press—he was persnickety about his coffee—and added two teaspoons of sugar, real sugar, no fake stuff, and a dollop of cream. Finding the breakfast tray in its usual place, she loaded up and carried it in to him, where he was already waiting, propped against the headboard, the sheet a pup-tent below his waist.

"Good morning," the Fat Girl said, and she set the tray between them. On her knees, she kissed him deeply and felt his hands grasp both of her breasts, her flesh spilling out between his fingers. Smiling at him, she took his sourdough toast, then plastered it over her breasts, smearing the jelly and the butter in a trail over both, and gliding down. It was Mark that moved aside the tray and then helped himself to her table. The Fat Girl knew what he liked. She knew what he wanted for breakfast. She'd been with him way more than one time. She was not alone. As the jelly lapped off her skin and onto Mark's warm and probing tongue, the Fat Girl thought how she had never been so happy. And when Mark moved over her and she opened herself to him, she decided it was in her nature to be so. They moved together and she was delirious.

Afterwards, Mark ate his cold omelet and then placed his hand on her thigh. The Fat Girl shifted, ready, expecting an encore performance. "We have to talk some, babe," he said.

He told her about the other woman. Actually, he told the Fat Girl that she was the other woman; that the first woman was his fiancée, and he was due to get married in a couple weeks, so their Friday nights together at his apartment were over. "Maybe we can meet at your place on some afternoons," he said, "if I can get off work." He showed her a picture of the fiancée. One glance told the Fat Girl that this woman would never be a customer at Large & Luscious.

The Fat Girl felt splattered like cracked eggs on the sheets. Her skin shifted and drooped, her breasts became thrown dough, her thighs a mass of fork-drawn creases. When she got out of bed, she tried desperately to cover herself.

"But why," she asked, tears pooling on her fat cheeks, her nose running, "why did you want me?"

"Oh, babe," he said and sighed deeply, rubbing his belly. "You know. It's so good! You know how good it is!"

She choked on her words. "More cushion, less pushin'?"

He smiled and let his hand drop invitingly to his crotch. She watched, and then went under for one last time. One last time of giving herself, opening herself, crying out, dreaming of large white wedding gowns and a blue paradise where she could be loved. Where the Fat Girl could be loved just like any other woman.

When she left that day, carrying her purse filled with weddings and honeymoons, she moved slowly with the careful step of used goods. It wasn't the move, it was the nature of the move. The Fat Girl left behind her address, written on a napkin smeared with mixed fruit jelly, on the breakfast tray.

THE FAT GIRLS AND THE SEVEN BOWLS

And I heard a loud voice from the temple, saying to the seven messengers, "Go on and pour out into the land the seven bowls of God's anger. —Revelations 16:1-17

MONDAY

The first angel went and poured out his bowl on the land, and ugly and painful sores broke out on the people who had the mark of the beast and worshiped his image.

Monday's Fat Girl wished she was a Medusa with snake arms instead of snake hair. It was her turn to grab the coffee and morning treats for her co-workers at the Large & Luscious Large Women's Clothing Boutique in the mall, so she threw her jacket over one shoulder, her purse over another, and her left hand held a drink carrier with three lattes and a cappuccino (cinnamon dolce, white chocolate, peppermint, and pumpkin spice). A bag filled with a cheese danish, a doughnut, and a piece of pumpkin bread was tucked in her armpit, while her right hand tried to grasp a paper bowl of hot oatmeal without squishing it or burning her fingers. Large & Luscious's glass doors were unlocked, but barely cracked open to keep early shoppers out and allow the Fat Girls in. The Fat Girl tried to nudge it the rest of the way with her foot when the door slid suddenly and she spun sideways. Lattes and cappuccino flew about her head and sent multiple shades of brown spatters to her sweater and slacks. The oatmeal, of course, split open when it landed on the floor, and the pastry bag spat out its contents as well. Mall walkers, going by at a fast clip, kicked the danish, the doughnut and the pumpkin bread like stones, sending crumbs and chunks and glazed sugar everywhere.

In the middle of it all, the Fat Girl lay flat out on her tummy, arms and legs extended into a treasure map X. Her lungs emptied by the force, she struggled to breathe as she watched all the sneakered feet going by.

One man, in a rhythm just beneath a jog, glanced down, and then at the Fat Girl. "Well, didn't you get yours," he called. And over his shoulder, "Suck it up! It all ends up in the same place anyway—your fat ass!"

The rest of the clerks and the store manager came running to the Fat Girl's rescue. Leaving her jacket and purse in the slop, the Fat Girl pushed painfully to her knees and accepted their hands and arms as she got to her feet. But then she walked straight through to the back of the store, into Fitting Room Number 7, and locked the door. Sitting down, she looked at her reflection in the mirror. Her cheeks were bright red, and she knew it was from anger at the almost-jogging man. Anger at all of them, at all those colorful striped and patterned and marching feet, not even pausing, not even breaking stride. But then the Fat Girl looked closer, and like milk into coffee, she felt the red of her anger drain to the pink of humiliation. She was brown-speckled and tan-spotted, her hair spun loose and damp from the flying coffees, and despite the care she took in her dressing that morning, she still looked fat. She noticed in particular the way her hips sloped down on either side of her, like foothills forming at her base. Fat ass. She stared and she stared as the other Fat Girls tapped on the fitting room door, asking if she was all right, asking if the spilled coffee burned her, if she hurt herself when she fell. She saw the color in her cheeks deepen again. Deepen and then sink into her pores, into the pools beneath her eyes.

Eventually, the manager got down on her hands and knees and peeked under the door. "You okay? We sent someone else for the breakfast."

The Fat Girl twitched and opened her arms.

The manager nodded. "I'll get you another sweater. You'll be fine. You can brush off the knees of your pants."

But the Fat Girl wasn't fine. At least she was able to clean up, and by the time she came out of the dressing room, the mess was gone and the store was fully open. New cups of coffee and a bowl of oatmeal and a bag of pastries waited on the counter. The baristas sent it all free of charge, the Fat Girl was told, because it wasn't fair that she and the others didn't get theirs. The Fat Girl thought she saw the almost-jogger go by again, fully dressed now and wearing black loafers, glancing and grinning her way, but she wasn't sure.

At home that night, she started to prepare her planned supper of a baked chicken breast and some vegetable soup, but when she opened her cupboard door to pull out some spices, she saw instead another mountain. This one was of Spaghetti-O's, a mix of the frank-filled and meatball varieties. They were on sale last week at the supermarket, ten for ten bucks, and so she bought ten of each kind. She was excited at the time; the store gave her what she deserved for being such a good customer, she shopped there all of time. It was like the Fat Girl received a reward. Now she stared at the colorful mountain for a bit, saw the reflection of her reflection in her mind. And then she put the chicken breast back into the refrigerator. She reached for her prize. She deserved it, after all.

Getting out her largest mixing bowl, she filled it with can after can after can of the Spaghetti-O's. For a few minutes, her kitchen was alive with the hungry buzz of the electric can opener and the metallic slurp of released noodles and tomato sauce. She heated it all in the microwave and then ate in front of the television. But at the end of the night, when she realized it was time for bed, she couldn't remember anything that she watched. She only remembered spoonfuls. Noodle after sauce after frank after meatball, into her mouth and onto the journey, mixing and mushing together, to all end up in the same place. Sucked up. Straight to her fat ass.

She'd stained the new sweater that the manager passed under the fitting room door. There were patches and streaks and smears of red, fading into a pinky-orange. Here and there, a noodle O straggled, malformed and hollow chicken pox. The sweater was white. And it wasn't even on sale. The manager might have allowed her to return it if it hadn't been messed up, if she'd taken it right off at home and gotten into something of her own. But now, there was no choice. It would come, of course, out of her paycheck and there would be a discount, but the sweater would likely never come clean. It would end up stuffed in the back of her closet or crammed one night into the garbage. She deserved it, of course. She was the one who hadn't taken care of it.

As far as the Fat Girl was concerned, the sweater could go straight to Hell. She slid her hand around the smooth side of the bowl, filling her fingers and knuckles and palm with red and orange. Then she rubbed her hand over herself, over her breasts, her stomach, down her sides, over her hips. She finger-painted with sauce until the sweater was covered, trailing and oozing everywhere, no pattern, no logic. After placing the bowl and her spoon into the dishwasher, she went to bed. Fully dressed. It could all go straight to Hell. Her fat ass could go straight to Hell. The Fat Girl could go straight to Hell. It was what she deserved, of course.

Her stomach moaned all night, and she had to get up three times to take a Rolaids.

But she got hers. She knew the almost-jogging man would think so. And she thought so too. She got hers.

TUESDAY

The second angel poured out his bowl on the sea, and it turned into blood like that of a dead man, and every living thing in the sea died.

Tuesday's Fat Girl dressed neatly in Large & Luscious clothes and pulled her hair back into a low ponytail. She loved the morning; going in to the mall before it was busy, ducking into the store before anyone else was allowed. It felt like a privileged time, like she was important and special and in on a secret nobody else knew. Except for her group, of course, the group of Fat Girls that worked at the store alongside her. The Fat Girl enjoyed being part of a secret; it made her feel like family. Once, when the Fat Girl was involved in one of those diet programs where you had to check in every other day and get weighed and have your food diary gone over like a master plan gone wrong, her diet instructor told her one of their secrets. A Skinny Girl secret.

"You know what we do on Saturdays sometime?" she asked. "Before all of you show up? One of us stops at a bakery and we have doughnuts and crème puffs for breakfast." She laughed. "We hide them in a closet so you guys will never see. Though we wonder sometimes if you'll sniff them out. Discover our dirty little secret like bloodhounds."

The Fat Girl quit the program that day.

At work during the pre-open hour, the Fat Girl always thought of that diet instructor as she waited by the cash register with the others for breakfast to arrive. Everyone took turns with the Starbucks run and the Fat Girl always enjoyed her peppermint latte and doughnut. The day before, their breakfast ended in disaster as one of the girls was knocked down with the order and by the time the others got to her, everything was pulverized and the fallen was struck silent and tearful. But today, Tuesday, they could tease her gently, and they did, remarking on her ballet twirl and gymnastic tumble, and the Fat Girl was thrilled to see her friend smile. The Fat Girl knew what it was like. She knew how it could be. But sitting there, in their secret enclave, the beautiful clothes around them neat and orderly, the counter clean, the carpet swept, the dressing rooms empty, the world locked away outside, they could all smile, and they did, and the Fat Girl loved it.

At noontime, the Fat Girl was the first to go on break and she grabbed a fashion magazine from her purse and went to the food court. She chose a garden salad and a cup of broccoli cheese soup and a diet soda from Quizno's. Her usual table near the outer edge of the food court was empty and the Fat Girl settled over her lunch, opening her magazine, curious to find what the fashions would be for winter. The white noise of the mall blew around her and she relaxed.

Eventually, strange hoots infiltrated her attention. She looked up and saw a group of ten teenagers at a round table nearby. They laughed and gestured in her direction, and one boy opened his mouth, wagging his tongue and showing her what was probably pizza. It seemed vaguely obscene, vaguely sexual, and the Fat Girl returned quickly to her magazine. But she couldn't concentrate.

She didn't understand how kids could come to a mall during lunch on a weekday. When she was in high school, the campus was closed; she and her friends couldn't leave for lunch without written permission from their parents. Besides, nobody had a car. Nobody had money to spend on food court food. They all either brown-bagged it or ate hot lunch.

For all four years of high school, the Fat Girl and her friends had their own table, as far away from the lunch line as they could get. Just like now. If there was going to be a spill, it seemed to happen soon after leaving the cashier, and so they were usually out of the line of fire. Old habits die hard. There were six girls in her group, no boys, except intermittently when one of them went out more than once with a certain guy. The Fat Girl had loved her friends, she saw them every day, spoke with them on the phone at night, coordinated her clothes with theirs. They were arm in arm in their graduation pictures, grinning, wearing bright purple robes and mortar boards. The Fat Girl's had a special tassel, and a gold cord hung around her shoulders, because she was an honor student.

The Fat Girl didn't know where that photo was now. She and her friends vowed to stay close, to be each others' bridesmaids, babysit for each others' children, gossip about each others' husbands. But it just hadn't happened that way. The Fat Girl knew where the others were; their information and occupations were proudly stated in the booklet that came every five years with an invitation to a reunion. There was a lawyer, an accountant, a make-up artist, a teacher, and a stockbroker. There were husbands and children. The Fat Girl, the honor student, had her degrees too, in math, but she worked as a sales clerk at Large and Luscious. She didn't go to the reunions. Her name, in the booklet, just gave her address and then had the initials NI. No Information.

A thunk on her table caused the Fat Girl to jump. A tray, then another and another and another, layered themselves until the entire table was covered. The Fat Girl looked up into the ten faces of teenage boys and girls. They beamed.

"We think it's a sin to waste food," one boy said, the one who had waved at her with his tongue. "So we figured you could finish up for us."

They laughed in unison and walked away, a collection of football jerseys and rock band t-shirts, cheerleader skirts and knee-baring blue jeans. Boys and girls alike wore backwards baseball caps.

The Fat Girl looked at the spoils. Pizza crusts, bits of ketchup, pulled-out pickles, overcooked fries. People at the surrounding tables glanced over, then returned to their meals. The Fat Girl saw secret smiles.

When she got up, the Fat Girl carefully extracted her tray from beneath all the others and carried it to the trash bin. She started to leave, but then she couldn't. She knew the food court custodians, and it just didn't seem fair to leave them with the work. All the work that was left for her, on her own table. The one she sat at, by herself, every day. Tray by tray, she emptied the trash. Partway through, one of the custodians joined her, gave her a weak smile, shrugged, and carried the junk alongside her. When the Fat Girl left, it looked like no one had been sitting there at all. The custodian gave the table a quick shiny wash-down.

At work that afternoon, one of the girls said that a restaurant in town was trying a Tuesday Night All You Can Eat Fish Fry. She invited the daytime Fat Girls to go, and they all agreed, even the manager. Two got off work at four, the Fat Girl and another at five, and the manager at six. They agreed to meet at the restaurant.

At first, it was fun. The Fat Girl sat there, surrounded by her friends, her co-workers, and they laughed and talked about the customers that day, about the girls working at night. There were no boys, just the five girls. They each wore trendy clothes from the boutique, their colors were bright, their hair done. Three out of the five had polished nails, and the other two were at least neatly trimmed. They were seated at a table in the middle of the restaurant, a table intended for eight. Yet the girls sat elbow to elbow.

The Fat Girl sat and listened to the chimes of her friends' laughter, and she joined in as well, leaning forward on the table. The waitress brought the first round of fried fish and they all began to eat, sharing the french fries set out and refilled in a basket in the middle. The crunch of batter was like walking through snow.

But then the Fat Girl heard an undertone. Whispers that weren't really whispers. Three tables had been pushed together nearby, tables meant for four each, but with their sides joining, they only accommodated eight total instead of twelve. The seven adults and one child, sitting there, stared at the five Fat Girls, at the table that should have been meant for them, for their party of eight. A table that now overflowed with a party of five. The Fat Girl and her friends continued to eat, but the Fat Girl dropped out of the conversation. She thought of that family, how they would have curled around the table for eight, talking and laughing, the mother and grandmother alternately wiping the child's face without having to lean away from the discussion. And she thought of herself and her friends, pulling up a chair, smushing around a table meant for four, a normal-sized four, separating the three tables lined up together now. That would have left two other tables for four free. The restaurant would have been able to serve eight more people than they were able to serve now. But because of them, because of the Fat Girl and her friends, their five bodies massed comfortably around the table for eight, the restaurant wasn't doing as well as it could be.

And she thought of the ten teens in the food court. The sin of wasted food.

The waitress showed up to serve the family, and then returned to the Fat Girl and her friends. The family bit into their first helping, what would undoubtedly be for some the last helping, as the waitress filled the Fat Girls' plates with their third.

As her friends talked and then pushed away their plates, the Fat Girl accepted a fourth.

And a fifth. A sixth. A seventh.

Her friends fell silent. The family of eight finished and left, and three groups of four came in and filled the split-apart tables, and then they left, and a group of six came in and took up two tables and one table stayed free. The Fat Girl's teeth began to hurt, her jaw to stiffen. Her skin felt stretched to impossible proportions and her fingers refused to bend. Her stomach hurt. Oh, it hurt. Sweat ran down the Fat Girl's forehead, blending with the tears on her cheeks and she ate some more. She asked for coleslaw.

Finally, the manager leaned forward, touched the Fat Girl's wrist. "Honey," she said. "Honey, that's enough."

The Fat Girl looked up. Crumbs sprinkled her chin and her cleavage, bits of cabbage and drips of mayo lined her lap. The restaurant was mostly empty. Her friends were staring, their plates cleared away. A waiter, who long since replaced the waitress, stood by her side, an empty basket in his hands. "I think you ate all the fish," he said. "All the fish in the sea." And then he guffawed.

The Fat Girl blushed and pushed back her chair. As the others walked away, she quickly wrote a check, leaving a tip for one-hundred and five dollars. Each patron, she knew, paid seven dollars for the all you can eat special. And she figured, with all the chairs that could have been filled if they had just sat at a table for four, with an extra chair added, that they cheated the restaurant out of at least fifteen customers. Fifteen times seven. One-hundred and five. She'd eaten their fish, it was a sin to waste food, and now she had to pay so the restaurant wouldn't be out the cash. It should all be even. It should all be fair. The Fat Girl left, walking bent over.

"Good grief," one of her friends said in the parking lot. "What got into you?"

"Besides fish," another said, but no one laughed.

The Fat Girl just shook her head. She couldn't speak. She knew if she opened her mouth, she would vomit.

Driving away, the Fat Girl watched her friends in the rearview mirror. They stood in a square, talking, gesturing, and they grew smaller and smaller until the night took them away. If only it was that easy. The Fat Girl's stomach, folded up and pressed against the steering wheel, rose up to her throat and threatened to spill over.

At home, the Fat Girl considered letting herself throw up. But she wouldn't give herself the pleasure.

WEDNESDAY

The third angel poured out his bowl on the rivers and springs of water, and they became blood.

Wednesday's Fat Girl had the day off and she took her time getting up in the morning. She had trouble sleeping the night before, picturing over and over her friend shoving battered fish into her mouth. The Fat Girl hadn't known what to do; no one had. They just watched with a fascination that seemed endless. When the Fat Girl had finally fallen asleep, she had nightmares of dead fish, entire oceans of dead fish, and all the Fat Girls from Large & Luscious were there, panning through the oceans like panning for gold, scooping the bodies up and dumping them right into huge openings in their own stomachs. They all had flaps, like trash containers. When she woke, the Fat Girl stared at the ceiling and she could still hear the susurrus of the ocean, the squeak and clap of the trash flap, and the slurp as fish after fish after fish was disposed of.

The Fat Girl sat up and looked out her window. It was sunny. The sky was blue too, one of those days where there weren't any clouds and she didn't miss them. The blue was enough. The Fat Girl wasn't particularly hungry (she wanted to laugh, thinking of all the dead fish she ate in her dream; she probably wouldn't be hungry for days). So she went to her closet and pulled out a pair of jazz pants and a favorite t-shirt. It was just plain, but a bright yellow, and the Fat Girl always felt shiny in it. She struggled into her sneakers and then pulled her hair into a sloppy bun, up off her neck.

In the kitchen, she pulled out a bottled water and drank most of it. Then she pulled out two more and clasped them like dumbbells. Her keys went into a secret pocket in her pants. And then she rolled out the door.

When the Fat Girl selected her apartment, she did so mostly because of the proximity to the Fox River. Just across the street was a lovely riverwalk, going several city blocks, then over a bridge, and up the other side. Walking by the Fox was restful and it made the simple exercise more fun. The Fat Girl could think, she could watch the water, count the ducks, admire the dragonflies, the cattails. She could study the ramp set up in the middle of the river for the city's waterskiing team and wonder what it must be like to skid seamlessly out of the water, up a ramp, into the air, and then splash right back down again. She imagined it must be like being a waterfowl, able to skim a watery surface and fly through the air.

Late on a mid-week morning, the Fat Girl had the riverwalk pretty much to herself. There were a few strollers, but more sitters, facing the river on wrought iron benches. The Fat Girl concentrated on her steps. One, two, one, two. The sky was blue, her shirt was yellow, and her sneakers set off a steady, clappable rhythm. She began alternating her water bottles, lifting each one opposite her step. Left leg, right arm, right leg, left arm. This added complication pleased her. She liked to keep her mind busy. When it was busy, it didn't wander. She began to sweat. She pictured her dream's tummy trash can sealed up tight, fish swimming whole out of her pores, wriggling across the walk and the grass and diving into the river, soon to find their way back to the ocean.

By the bridge, there was a circular set of cement steps leading down to the water for those that wanted to fish. On this day, there was a group of five men and one woman, all older, all probably retired. They sat cross-legged on the ground or in lawn chairs, some with several fishing poles dangled into the water and weighted on the concrete. There were red and green coffee cans everywhere and the Fat Girl assumed they were full of bait. Bright red coolers reminded her of Christmas presents.

As if they heard her coming, the fishing people turned and looked at her. She waved, calling out, "Lovely day!" They didn't respond, just watched her walk up the slight

Enlarged Hearts

incline to the bridge, cross over it, and then down the other side. She knew they were watching, she could feel it and hear the buzz of their voices, and it reminded her of something. Of parading? Parading at night? She felt wet and exposed and she ducked, but then she realized the incline had turned her sweat into a sheet and she was okay. For a moment, she stopped her weight lifting and instead ran a water bottle across her forehead. Then she uncapped one and drank, stepping in place. This made her dumbbells out of balance and so she opened the other bottle and drank an equal amount from that one. Then she set off again, lighter water bottles raising and lowering, raising and lowering. Right leg, left arm.

The fishing woman called, "Two-fisted drinker, huh?" and smiled. The Fat Girl laughed and raised one bottle in salute. "Good for you," the woman said.

One of the men snorted. "Two-fisted eater too, I bet," he said. The other men grunted in what might have been laughter. "Your thunder is scarin' the fish."

Thunder. Thunder and lightning. The room lit up like a disco. Her body moving in a bizarre dance that she didn't understand. Men. Boys. Her age.

"Frank!" the woman scolded and all the men stared at the river. She looked back at the Fat Girl, at a dead stop with her bottles dangling at her thighs. "Don't you listen, hon," she said. "You keep going. You go, girl!"

The Fat Girl did. She rolled her thunder, her feet getting heavier and heavier. She thought of the fish in the river, feeling her reverberation, swimming away, scared. Of her. She remembered being scared, she remembered running away. She remembered being caught, and the thunder and the disco. The ducks seemed to swim away too. And there weren't any dragonflies. Two-fisted eater. She thought of her friend. Of her own fat hands wrapped around beer-battered fish, filling and emptying three plates. She thought of all the fish in the ocean, of the waiter standing there, with his empty basket, saying, "I think you ate all the fish in the sea."

Left leg, right arm. Right leg, left arm.

She remembered the lights in the disco. She remembered all the dark corners and the boys there. The thunder of her own feet. The silence when she stopped. The bizarre dance that she'd never known before.

When she got back to her apartment, the Fat Girl was soaked. She threw her bottles in the sink and tossed off her clothes as she headed for the bathroom. She turned the cold water on full blast and stood under the shower until she began to shiver. Her teeth chattered.

Two-fisted eater.

And that was, after all, what she was. Two-fisted eater. Two-mouthed. She did it all. She took it all in. Right hand, left hand. Bizarre dance, clappable rhythm.

She turned on the hot water tap and closed her eyes until she stopped shivering. Then she looked down.

Her breasts, smooth rolling flesh, nestled on her belly. Without the support of a bra, her breasts had no life. The only touch they felt, the only skin to skin, was with her own stomach, and with her own hands when she lifted each to wash beneath. Her stomach rolled out too, rubbery and wicked. The Fat Girl traced her fingers down. Down a slope, into a tuck. Down a slope, into a tuck. The last ended at her thighs. Her fingers had to become excavators then, lifting and plowing into a solid wall to find what was under. She knew her sex was under there somewhere, but she hadn't really thought about it for a while, she kept her mind busy, only paying attention when the intermittent bleeding came, when she cushioned her deepest self in pads, feeling, sometimes, like she was diapering a baby. Or like she was plugging a hole in the dam.

She was roll upon roll upon roll. Layer upon layer. Secret after secret after secret.

But it's who she was. She liked to keep her mind busy. Left foot, right foot.

She didn't understand it any more than anyone else. She'd done the diet route, the therapy route, the hypnosis route. And here she was. She was here, somewhere. Beneath the layers. Still. Forever.

She was thunder. She was a horror movie. People looked away. She scared the fish.

The Fat Girl was gross. And she knew it.

It wasn't what she intended. She intended the opposite. Buried under layers. Who could see?

The warm water turned her body red now, though the Fat Girl knew it wasn't all from the heat. I'm sorry, she thought. I'm so sorry. I don't mean to offend. I've never meant to offend.

She hung her head.

She was layer after layer. She was an onion. Raising her head, she realized. The secrets were supposed to be inside, she was supposed to be on the outside. She'd gone the wrong way. Instead of burying the secrets, she'd buried herself. She was inside out. No wonder.

She picked up her razor and then she hefted her left foot onto the tub's edge. Her big toe was the easiest to reach and so she pressed the razor against the side of it and drew down.

The disco ball.

And again.

The dark corners, the lights splashed in her eyes. The hands.

And again.

The hands. The boys. She ran. And then she stopped.

Again.

The dance. The dance and the dance and the dance.

The water turned pink and the skin ran down the drain, her toe seemed to slim down. She peeled back the layers. She exposed. Washed it away.

When the pain became too great, she shifted to the other foot.

After her shower, she bandaged her lesser self carefully, gently. She tried using gauze, but they soaked through. Finally, she gave up and pulled out a package of Kotex. She wrapped one pad around each foot, the bulk by the big toes, and taped them in place. For Wednesday, her day off, it would do.

And so it would go, she decided. Each day, a layer gone, a new layer exposed. She would make amends. She never intended to offend. She didn't mean to make people mad. She was mad too, and she would rectify the situation. It would take a while, she thought, but if she used something bigger than a razor and if she stripped a layer each day, starting at her neck and going down to her feet and working her way around her huge body, her gross body, then by the time she got back to where she began, the original slices should be healed and she could start all over again.

All over. Until she'd shaved off all the excess and there she'd be, just herself, and no one would mind her existence. It might take months. But she would still be here. The secrets would be gone. No one would know. Forever.

She took a painkiller and then dressed neatly, in jeans and another t-shirt, not-so-favorite, but close. She padded around barefoot, her toes wads of cotton, and figured if she went out, she'd have to wear sandals. She could say she had foot surgery. She felt good. The anger had drained, it seemed, with the blood. And maybe the secrets too.

But later, when she went back in the bathroom for more painkillers, the pink streaks in the tub and the soaked pads on her feet made her retch.

THURSDAY

The fourth angel poured out his bowl on the sun, and the sun was given power to scorch people with fire.

Thursday's Fat Girl wasn't supposed to be at the store on Thursday. She was supposed to be at school. She was the hired-for-the-summer Fat Girl, now transitioning into being a weekend Fat Girl because school resumed. But when the manager called and said someone was sick, and she'd called everyone and no one else could fill in, and the Fat Girl heard the desperation in the manager's voice, the Fat Girl lied. Out of earshot of her mother. The Fat Girl said she didn't have school because of teacher's convention and that she would be happy to fill in. The manager's relief made the Fat Girl feel so good, as if she were a superhero, someone who had just allayed a crisis situation.

The Fat Girl left her home right on time that morning, carrying her backpack, but instead of walking to school, she went around the block and got on the city bus heading to the mall. She used her cell to call the school office and she disguised her voice to sound like her mother. She gave herself strep throat. Everyone had strep throat. Then she went to the mall's food court, open early for the mall workers and walkers, and had McDonald's for breakfast. The Big Breakfast platter, with pancakes and eggs and sausage and hash browns, and a big cup of premium coffee. It was so much better than the two brown sugar cinnamon Pop Tarts she had at home, and the hot chocolate, because her mother insisted she was too young for coffee. She was sixteen, for crap's sake!

When the Fat Girl slipped in between the barely cracked doors of the store, the manager eyed her backpack. "I thought there wasn't any school," she said.

"There isn't," the Fat Girl lied. "But there's still homework, so I figured I'd work on that during lunch."

The manager nodded. The Fat Girl figured she just scored points for being responsible.

The Fat Girl loved being at the store. She couldn't wait for another year and a half, when she would graduate, and hopefully come here to work full-time. And then she could maybe go to tech school too, part-time. Her mom didn't have the money to pay her tuition and her dad was useless. She only saw him once a month and they spent the whole weekend in his apartment, sitting on the couch, watching television. Well, he watched television. The Fat Girl watched the clock, waiting for Sunday night at five so she could go home.

The Fat Girl wanted to be a fashion designer. She thought that working at the store full time while going to school part time would look good on her future resume. And she really loved it here anyway. The Fat Girls all liked her. They thought she was cute. And she thought so too. Now, anyway. Since coming to the store.

After stowing her backpack in the storeroom, the Fat Girl went to work without being told what to do. She knew everything had to be straightened, even though the night girls cleaned up before they went home. They had to check and double-check. Sizes in order, clothes according to style and color, hangers untangled and all going the same way. The Fat Girl knew that in a few minutes, one of the other girls would elbow her way in through the doors, bringing everyone Starbucks. That's why the Fat Girl had her breakfast down in the court. She wasn't usually here, not on a schoolday morning, and so she figured they would forget her.

But they didn't. What a surprise! Her co-worker brought her a peppermint mocha latte, her favorite, and sparkly white mini-doughnuts. The Fat Girl was more than full, but she ate it anyway. She didn't want to hurt any feelings, and it was so cool that they remembered. She always remembered friends' birthdays at school. And favorite colors. And what sport or activity everyone did, and who was going with who and who just broke up. They never remembered her stuff. But then, things would be changing soon. She only hung by them now. They weren't used to the difference yet. School only started a month ago.

They would notice soon enough. Like the Fat Girls did. She was cute. Her sweat pants and stretch pants were all in the back of her closet. So were her dumpy t-shirts. She'd bloomed! That's what her mother said anyway. She wore glorious shirts now, peasant-style, gathered below her boobs, flowing material, bell sleeves, great detail. A little tie in the back. Scoop neck, and her breasts suddenly crested the shirts' horizons, two tanned planets, threatening to fall out of orbit if she bent too low or pulled the shirts down too quickly. Mid-rise snug fit jeans, which, when she stretched for something or tilted just the right way, exposed her tummy, rounding over the waistband. The Fat Girl's skin was smooth and pink and sweet. She knew the other girls at school, at least some of them, had concave tummies, their pelvic bones thrusting out like buck teeth, gaps in the waistbands of their jeans just inviting a thrust hand. But the Fat Girl, in these lovely new clothes, looked like a buffet, she thought. Rich. Overflowing. Not fat, really, but bounteous.

The Fat Girl, at night, dreamed of being reveled in. Feasted on. Oh, enjoyed. When the boys finally turned their eyes away from skin'n'bones and saw her, saw the luxury, their eyes would pop. She was cute. She was more than cute. She wasn't quite sure what she was, but she was ready to be told.

After breakfast, the Fat Girl helped the others bring out the new clothes for the winter and holiday line-up. It was a great day to be here, to see firsthand the new styles and materials, to touch them before anyone else did. The Fat Girl loved the colors. Vibrant oranges and reds and deep chocolate browns. Jewel tones in red and green.

"Sweetheart," the manager said, interrupting the Fat Girl's latest examination of a blouse. "Remember, you're not shopping. You're working."

The Fat Girl smiled and resumed hanging shirt after shirt, sweater after sweater. She would be shopping, she knew. Right when work ended and before she went home. She needed to package herself for the holidays, warm herself for the winter.

When the manager went to lunch, she assigned the Fat Girl to the cash register. The Fat Girl was honored; the cash register was a premier spot. It was like the throne of the store. Being trusted with the money was a huge statement.

For a while, the Fat Girl looked at a fashion magazine. Then she checked the day's total intake so far; four-hundred dollars. Not bad for a weekday by noon, she thought, feeling professional. Then she settled back in the chair to watch the other girls. There were two of them out in the store, both of them seasoned employees. One was the Fat Girl's mother's age and the Fat Girl was amazed, sometimes, at how much more comfortable she was with this Fat Girl than with her mother. She loved her mother, of course, but there was this sense of camaraderie with the other employees. Sharing the same goals, the same passion. Fashion, making women look good, the whispering and giggles behind the scenes. They had the most fun when they were setting up a display for new underwear.

The Fat Girl watched one of the others helping a customer. They were sorting through the colorful long-sleeved t-shirts set out on a table, new for the winter. The customer was quite large, and they had to dig deep for her size. The Fat Girl made a note for herself to check that table later; she'd invented a new policy of putting at least one stack of clothes out with the largest sizes on top, so that the larger customers didn't feel like they had to dig down to the bottom of the pile, the dregs, to get to what fit them. The Fat Girl brought it up at the last staff meeting and the manager thought it was a wonderful idea. It wasn't routine yet, though, so the Fat Girl made it her responsibility to check.

The customer dropped a shirt and the other Fat Girl stooped to pick it up. She wore a crossover blouse that tied on the side and when she bent, her breasts surged forward. The Fat Girl stifled an urge to giggle. But then she noticed the creases. The other girl's cleavage puckered and crinkled, looking like a mud puddle on a windy day. The breasts swayed and rippled, not held in place even by the supportive bra she wore.

The Fat Girl glanced down at herself. Her breasts were smooth, there was nothing but round and pink. But when she glanced back and forth, between the other Fat Girl and herself, she saw that they were about the same size.

The Fat Girl put a protective hand over her cleavage.

Shifting away, the Fat Girl looked instead at the clerk dressing the mannequins filling the ledge that ran around three walls of the store. One ledge was for more formal wear, dresses and such, especially during the holidays. The other two ledges showed casual wear and sleepwear.

The Fat Girl couldn't help but notice, in profile, how the other girl's butt swelled, out of proportion with the rest of her body. It looked like someone stuck twin watermelons down her pants. The Fat Girl had heard the term bubble-butt, but this ass was no bubble. And the front of her pants, exposed when the other Fat Girl stretched up, looked like a sack of potatoes against her thighs. The Fat Girl was tempted to giggle again, until she noticed the wide strip of skin above the other girl's waistband.

Well, there was no waistband. Or there was, but it was buried. The other Fat Girl's stomach rolled out over her pants, with a deep crease in the side where the waistband cut in. This Fat Girl's tummy looked like a rotted side of ham, a mottled pink and silver and red-streaked mass. It crumpled and dimpled, and swung slowly back and forth like…The Fat Girl blushed. The other girl's stomach looked like the scrotal sac the Fat Girl saw on the elephant at the zoo.

Up on her ladder, the other girl glanced over, then quickly tugged down her shirt. The Fat Girl felt suddenly embarrassed. And suddenly scared.

And suddenly sick.

At school the next day, the Fat Girl hung just outside the group of her friends. She wore a new shirt, a deep burnt orange, and dark low-rise jeans, bought yesterday before she left the store. Her new clothes held her in with stiffness and she couldn't help, every now and then, glancing down at her breasts, rising out of the deep V-neck.

Seeing that one of her sneakers needed tying, the Fat Girl set down her books and bent low. Two hands suddenly clasped her breasts like handles. She rose, these hands still on her, lifting her weight, lifting her. She looked into the face of a boy, who smiled and winked.

"Just helping you up," he said. His thumbs smoothed two circles on her bare skin. He squeezed.

The Fat Girl felt a rush of heat. She burned. And she didn't know what to do.

She heard laughter.

The boy let his hands drift as he stepped away, and he managed to grab each nipple, already raised, in a sharp tweak. "See you later," he said.

The Fat Girl watched him walk away. He joined another girl, her shirt still summer-short, and he tucked his hand into the gapping waistband of her jeans. His knuckles bulged through the denim.

And the Fat Girl burned, where he touched her. She burned, where he grasped the other. Standing by the row of lockers, all of them closed, the hall emptying, she burned in her new V-neck shirt, her low-rise jeans.

She was still there, when the bell rang, her books in a neat stack on the floor. She wasn't sure where to go.

FRIDAY

The fifth angel poured out his bowl on the throne of the beast, and his kingdom was plunged into darkness. Men gnawed their tongues in agony and cursed the God of heaven because of their pains and their sores, but they refused to repent of what they had done.

You are a Fat Girl, and you are proud of it. You tell yourself that you choose to be this way, and you really believe that you do. You are one of those Fat Girls that looks good, that carries her weight well, carries herself well. Your shoulders back, breasts thrust out, wide hips rolling with power. You dress well too, in clothes that fit and flow, bright colors that enhance here, tuck away there. You keep your hair styled, your fingers manicured, your neck, ears and wrists jeweled. There is no doubt, when you walk into a room, that you turn heads. You know it and you relish it.

You shop at the Large & Luscious Large Women's Clothing Boutique in the mall. You love this store, love the atmosphere, the fabrics, the styles. You enjoy catching the eye of another shopper and sharing a smile, both of you knowing that you are in a place where you belong, where others can't go, totally unlike those generic clothing stores that are for the general population. Here, you learn the tricks of the trade, and when you walk out with your bags, you know you will continue making a statement.

And that statement? Bold. Big is beautiful. Big is control and strength and intelligence and incredible, incredible power. You can squash people, just like that. You can squash men and women. You are the one in charge.

And yet there are the clothing details, the colors, the splash of pink or lilac, the image of a flower petal slipping over a breast, its tip ending just at your nipple. You can be soft too, and one hell of a wonder in bed. You know that you don't have to be bones to make a man's whole body stiff with desire. You've learned the tricks of the trade.

Around you, people verify your statement every day. You are in charge at work, you are in charge at home, you are in charge of your life. You always have more than your share of lovers. You aren't married yet, but not because there haven't been offers. You enjoy sharing your bed, then sending someone home so you can stretch out in all your glory and sleep in utter privacy, waking when you choose to.

On this day, you stop by at Large & Luscious after work. It's a Friday and you feel lazy, you don't want to go right home. You might even treat yourself to dinner out. But first, you want to look at the new line-up; you received the email announcement for the new winter and holiday line. You're sure that there will be something knock-out to wear to the office Christmas party and you want to grab it while it's hot on the rack. The party is always held in a chandelier-dripping ballroom and you anticipate your moment of entry, the quiet gasp from the women, the upraised eyebrows of the men. You are a stunner and you know it. You carry your weight well.

Going over to the formal wear, you start looking through the new assortment. There are the usual choices in black, but a red grabs your eye. The neck is draped and deep, the straps slim silver chains to show off your shoulders, the back low and bare, but criss-crossed with more silver chains, larger, and shiny. In the exact middle, a stunning jewel, a silver rose trimmed with red. You've never seen back jewelry before and this delights you.

A few feet over, a mother is shopping for a dress for her daughter. It's for Homecoming, you overhear in their conversation. In their argument; it escalates quickly. The girl looks at and pulls out dress after dress; when you glance their way, you see she's in the size eighteen section. The mother says, "Why can't you just lose weight? We've tried every diet there is, and still you're fat! We would have so many more choices at other stores. But you just eat and eat and eat and eat! You're a little pig! Don't you have any self-respect at all?"

The girl says nothing, just looks at another dress, an emerald green, beautiful, and pulls it out.

The mother fires a sigh, then turns away, saying, "You embarrass me. Really, you embarrass me." She catches you watching, looks down the expanse of your body, and shakes her head. Then she leaves.

The girl doesn't even pause in her search, her tears dotting the abundance of fabric in her arms. You bite your tongue and take your dress to the fitting room.

The dress goes easily over your head and skims your body like poured water. You straighten the straps and then turn to look at the back. The silver against your dark skin is stunning. The rose is an invitation for a hand, a gentle touch to lead you to the dance floor.

You will need silver heels.

Outside, you hear a clerk call to someone in a different dressing room. "How's it going in there?"

The answer is a sigh.

"Really," the clerk says. "I think it's so wonderful to be going on a Christmas cruise. And to Alaska! That's so exciting!"

The woman in the fitting room says, "I look terrible."

"Do you need another size?"

"No. I just look terrible." There is a flump and you know she just sat down on the bench.

"I'll be right back," the clerk says. "I think I have just the right thing for you. Really."

You take one more look at the dress, determine that it is as perfect as you thought it was on the first glance, then pull it over your head. You plan to stop at Payless ShoeSource on your way out, see if you can find the silver heels you want. Stiletto. Maybe with reflective chains on the straps. It's all in the details.

In the next room, you hear another sigh. And then softly, a whisper: "I hate this. Oh, I just hate this."

You bite your tongue and leave the fitting area. On the way, you pass the clerk, her arms filled with leggings and long tunic-style sweaters. You approve; it's a trick of the trade and they will look good. Then you head for the check-out.

As you wait, you thread through their jewelry. They always have some pretty things, but you never buy here. You prefer artist-made jewelry. You love the idea that whatever you wear, you are the only one wearing it.

There are two girls working check-out, the second at the cash register, the first accepting the clothes, removing the security strip, folding them onto pink tissue and placing them next to pink bags, ready to be tucked away after the price is rung up. The folder sees your dress and beams. "Isn't this beautiful?" she says. "We just got it in today, and as soon as I saw it, I was wowed."

"I fell in love with it too," you say. "Especially the rose on the back."

"It'll look great next to your skin tone," she says. "You can do justice to red and silver!"

The two customers ahead of you at the cash register are speaking in low tones, when suddenly, one leaps louder. She swings on the girls behind the desk. "How can you encourage this?" she says, gesturing to her companion. "She needs to lose weight, everyone who comes here, everyone who works here, needs to lose weight!" She expands her arms to the whole store, including you. "You're just letting them all stay fat, you're letting them all be weak and they're too stupid to see it. It's just not healthy!"

Her friend says, "Please, Amber, just—"

The woman faces into the store and yells, "You're all like cows at a trough!" She looks at you and you see her stop for a moment, her mouth still open. Then she says to her friend, "I'll meet you at the car. I can't stand watching you do this." She stops just outside the door and rummages through her purse. Before she steps away, heading to parking lot, she already has her cigarettes and lighter ready.

You bite your tongue.

"I'm sorry about that," the remaining woman says. "She means well. She really does care."

"It's okay," the cashier says. "We hear a lot of that."

You feel a sigh build and you let it out gently. No one hears.

Finally, you take your turn at the cash register. The cashier too comments on the beauty of the dress and how wonderful it will look on you. You stand tall, your shoulders back, chest raised, and you know you will. Look beautiful. You carry your weight well. The image you project is glorious. You know the tricks of the trade. It's all in the details.

You tell them it is for your office Christmas party and that you are off to find a pair of silver heels. Stilettos. Hopefully with a chain detail on the straps.

"Perfect," they say.

As you gather up your bag and head to the entry, one of the girls tells you to have a great day. "And a wonderful office party," she says.

You head toward the shoe store and you think about the party. You might be accompanied by whomever you're dating at the time. Or you might go solo. It's a large company and there are many men in other departments. Either way, you won't go home alone that night. In your bedroom, the dress will skim off as easily as it went on, and the stilettos just might stay on, or they might be off, or one might be on the floor while the other is still on your foot. You will roll around with this man in the fuzzy silver of the streetlight glow, you will roll around and moan and squeal, climax and make him climax too. Maybe more than once. And then he will dress while you pull on your silk robe, rich dark brown, delicious, and you will walk him to the door. In the dark, he will kiss you deeply, promise to call, and then the shock of light from the hallway will pour in, leaving a broad strip on the floor. The door will close, gently, and he'll be gone.

You'll return to your bedroom, let your robe slide like melted chocolate to the floor. Stepping into the bathroom, you will turn on the light. Your reflection will take up the mirror and you will stand there and stare.

And you will bite your tongue. Oh, you will bite your tongue.

SATURDAY

The sixth angel poured out his bowl on the great river Euphrates, and its water was dried up to prepare the way for the kings from the East.

Saturday's Fat Girl had the weekend off, and she invited all the Fat Girls to her apartment for a casual dinner. She knew the ones scheduled to work would be late, but she promised she would save the leftovers, promised she would make a fresh batch of margaritas and cosmos when they arrived. The Miss America Pageant was on this night, and everyone wanted to see it.

The Fat Girl had a spacious apartment, one with a dining room, and she added two leaves to her table and set out the food a few minutes before anyone was due to arrive. Sliced ham and turkey and beef for sandwiches. Potato salad, cole slaw, macaroni salad, fruit fluff. Chips and dip. Crackers and cheese. A relish plate of black and green olives, baby carrots, raw broccoli, and cauliflower. And three trays of cookies and bars. She knew that, even though she told the girls not to, several would bring offerings of their own.

Right on time, the girls began to show up. Soon, ten Fat Girls crowded around the dining table, with four more due after store's closing. They laughed and chattered, filling their plates with a little bit of everything. The Fat Girl kept busy, alternating between the blender and the shaker, making margarita after margarita, cosmo after cosmo. By the time everyone was seated with full glasses and full plates, the pageant was ready to begin, and the Fat Girl was ready too. She filled her own plate, filled her own glass (a raspberry margarita), and then stood behind the couch. She balanced her plate on the couch's back, placed her drink on the nearby dining table. Several of the girls offered to scoot over or give her a chair, but she refused. From this vantage point, as if she was standing on a bridge over a great river, she could see everyone, and she could see the television, and she could be ready to grab something if someone needed it.

As the show started and the fifty-three contestants flowed across the stage, everyone leaned forward, including the Fat Girl. She rested her elbows on the back of the couch. She knew what everyone was hoping for. It was what she hoped for too. One contestant—just one—who was a Fat Girl. Or who was at least a rounded girl. A full girl. One, two, three…Alabama, Alaska, Arizona…on and on and on they went, a muted brilliance of pastels across the stage. The Fat Girl noticed there were no bold colors. Everything was frothy. Fluffy. Somehow hinting of pink even if it wasn't.

When Miss Wyoming took her turn, there was a collective sigh and a sitting back. The Fat Girl hurried to the kitchen for a refill of margaritas. They all knew what this meant. There still wasn't any change. Despite all the media hoo-ha on the exposed frail bones of models and celebrities, society's anxious awareness of anorexia and bulimia and their self-righteous declaration of a positive body image, the women chosen to represent each state, to represent beauty and poise and grace, were still tall and thin, thin, thin. None of those States would have ever crossed the threshold of Large & Luscious.

After another round of drinks, the living room seemed to relax. The ball gown event went by with plenty of admiration and comparisons of styles and fabrics. The Fat Girls talked about how this color or that style worked or didn't work on each individual State, and they also offered up how it would look on this Fat Girl or that. No one mentioned how the cuts would have to change. Then the talent competition went by with plenty of hoots of derision as the States dropped their batons, messed up on the piano, had pointe shoes fall off mid-leap. One girl lost her pigeons during a magic act. But there were plenty of gasps of pleasure too, over full and solid voices, violin solos, and one phenomenal reading of original poetry.

The four remaining Fat Girls showed up at nine-thirty, sharing a car and an appetite. They were just in time for the swimsuit event. Room was made on the floor for the new arrivals and they were quickly caught up on the pageant through a series of opinions and reports. The Fat Girl brought them plates filled with the leftovers and then took up her post behind the couch again. Her feet were beginning to hurt, but the only space left was on the floor and a good hostess never sat herself on the floor and the Fat Girl was always a good hostess. She had to be ready to serve. She wanted the Fat Girls to be comfortable. She wanted them to be happy.

The swimsuit event started after the commercial break. Bikini after tankini went by and the Fat Girl watched the thighs of her friends. One by one, each Fat Girl surreptitiously opened her legs, trying to see how far apart they would have to be before their thighs separated like Siamese twins in surgery. The Fat Girls on the couch had to test their own thighs one at a time, secretly, yet in cahoots with each other; there wasn't room for all of them to spread their fat legs at once. Even the Fat Girl steadied herself with her hands flat on the back of the couch and she slid her feet apart in the very beginning of a Chinese split. She had to hold herself up with her arms to keep her balance in order for her legs to expose her denim-clad crotch.

The States bubbled on stage with solid air between their thighs; the Fat Girl could see right between them, to the girls directly behind, waiting to start their sexy stroll. They wore high heels with their swimwear, and their feet crossed in front of each other, creating an easy and sensual hip swing. Most of the swimsuits looked like they would fall apart if they clad a slender body in actual water. The Fat Girl thought of the suits at the store; a riot of colors with built-in bras, pretty skirts meant to drift over dimpled thighs. Stripes and flowers, polka dots and palm leaves helped Fat Girls to blend into the water, join it, enhance it. On the television, there was mostly solid black, and of course, creamy skin.

At the end of the pageant, the winner was declared, and she was nobody's favorite. Not a single State was anyone's favorite, for that matter. There were no favorites. The television was turned off, and the Fat Girls sat in silence, wiping the dregs from their plates with single fingers and then popping them in their mouths.

The Fat Girl collected plates and cups and turned down offers to help clean up. She encouraged them all to just sit and relax and talk amongst themselves. The store's manager, sitting in a recliner in the corner, smiled and kicked her footrest in. She began talking about the new winter line-up, how excited the customers seemed to be, how clothes were literally just walking out the door. She usually didn't work on weekends, being the manager, but during the holiday season, nothing could keep her away. At one point that day, she said, there were women lined from the fitting rooms to the mall entry, waiting to try on armfuls of clothes. Another Fat Girl took over the story, explaining how she quickly ran to the Original Cookie Company and bought bags of their mini-cookies, bringing them back to the store to hand out to those in line. A third Fat Girl made a trip to Starbucks and came back with one of their Portable Party Coffeepots, complete with cups, and she passed those out too. The manager laughed and said it was like a party, a fashion show, as women in the dressing rooms stepped out to show off to those in line, and those in line chorused their comments and voted on their favorites.

It was just amazing, the manager said.

Alone in her kitchen, the Fat Girl sat on a stool and loaded her dishwasher while listening to the song of conversation. Trills of laughter, bass tones of consternation, rose up into an easygoing melody and accompanying harmony. The Fat Girl scraped, bent, and rose, raising a rhythm, and didn't stop until the job was done.

After turning on the dishwasher, the Fat Girl straightened and ran her hands through her hair. Arms upraised, hair held in a bunch off her neck, the Fat Girl caught a glimpse of herself in the window. Her cheeks were pink with exertion, her hair pleasantly messy. She found herself smiling. Her arms lifted her breasts, and while both her arms and breasts jiggled, they looked warm and welcoming. The window framed her like a photograph and the Fat Girl posed. She liked what she saw. Even though it was her weekend off, she wished she'd been to work that day, to see the impromptu party, the impromptu fashion show, the joining of ideas and opinions and laughter and just flat-out fun. It must have been wonderful.

The Fat Girl listened for a minute and realized the conversation had stopped. She returned to the living room and found her friends looking toward the blank TV. The Fat Girl could see their expressions in the screen and they weren't anything like what she just saw in her window. The manager had her feet up again, and her face was turned away, her body slumped. The Fat Girl knew she had to do something. She never wanted anyone to leave her apartment unhappy. And the Fat Girls…well, the Fat Girls were really the only ones who ever came to her apartment.

"Hey," the Fat Girl said. "I know it's cold, but let's go do something. Come with me. The lake is just a short walk from here. It's beautiful at night."

There was a group grump and the Fat Girl moved around the room, grabbing hands and pulling women to their feet. Some put up a fight, which brought laughter again, and the Fat Girl felt a profound sense of relief. She needed her friends to be happy. They had to be happy. What else was there?

After pulling on jackets and hats, yanking on mittens and tying scarves, the fifteen Fat Girls walked two abreast down the street. By herself, the Fat Girl led the way, a majorette at a parade, and the conversation ran up and down the line like music on an xylophone. They weren't worried about the late hour; they were a large body of women, they were safe and they were loud. For that walk, they didn't care what anyone thought. They were together and they enjoyed it.

Crossing the street and then a patch of frosted grass, the Fat Girl showed the others the long rickety flight of stairs leading down to the beach. "If we break it, who cares?" said the Fat Girl. "We'll just spend the night on the sand."

"Huddled together like a group of beached whales!" called another.

"Imagine the headlines," said a third. "Gruesome Discovery on Milwaukee Shores: A Herd of Beached Whales! No, Wait…They're Only Women!"

"Do whales travel in herds?" asked a fourth.

They all pondered that as they descended the stairs. Or at least, the Fat Girl did. She decided to google it when she got home. She wanted to know what they traveled in.

On the beach, the Fat Girls lined up, side by side, and faced the lake. Lake Michigan was already partly frozen over, at least by the shore, and the ice looked like a frozen desert, bumping with sand granules, as if the great lake had suddenly gone barren of water. Farther out, the white filigreed to gray and then to black, and the Fat Girl could hear the drone of waves, which muted rhythmically as they slid under the ice.

Standing there, the Fat Girl was, as usual, swept away by the lake. Lake Michigan, in winter or summer, was both inspiring and friendly. The Fat Girl liked to think of the waves as multitudes of shoulders, powerful shoulders, that ran to the beach and hugged her feet, or captured her whole, on the days that the waters were warm enough to swim in. Despite the expanse, despite the sheer hugeness of the lake, the Fat Girl always felt watched over, cradled, embraced. Now, of course, the rim was frozen and the Fat Girl looked longingly out to the open water, wishing she could touch it. Glancing down the long line of fifteen Fat Girls, all facing forward, all with red cheeks in the blue-cold wind, the Fat Girl wished they could feel what she did by Lake Michigan. She wished they could feel what she did when she saw her reflection in her kitchen window. And she wished their lives were always like it was at the store, particularly when customers stretched to the doorway, filled the dressing rooms, and shared their clothing choices with each other, and all rejoiced in their effulgence. In their solidarity and their independence, rolled together in a fat and warm sisterhood.

The Fat Girl took the hand of the Fat Girl next to her, and she saw her smile in the moonlight. That Fat Girl grasped the next, and so on, until they formed a chain. A chain of hands and a chain of smiles. Then the Fat Girl stuck out her leg, like a can-can dancer, and kicked her boot off. All the way down the line, boots and shoes can-canned off, creating a scattered row of zippers and straps and laces and soles in the sand. The Fat Girl waited until the last shoe settled on its side, and then she fell awkwardly back on her ass, yanking the next girl down with her, and all the others crashed down too, a wiggling mass of giggling Fat Girls.

The laughter subsided and they all lay flat on their backs. The stars were filled with bravado on this night and they balanced in the black sky like trophies on shelves, second, third, fourth, and millionth place. The moon was the crown jewel, the tiara, its glow a scepter.

The Fat Girl stuck her foot toward that moon and yanked her sock off, sending it to join the row of shoes. Down the line, the can-can struck back up, as argyles, prints, rainbows and lacy whites traveled down ankles and over toes and fluttered through the air and to the sand.

"Okay," the Fat Girl called. "Now stand up! Stand up!"

They did, balancing on one leg, dangling their feet, leaning on each other for support.

"Now go to the edge!" The Fat Girl started hopping, and for a moment, she was held back, the line resisting, moans hurtling toward the moon. But then they all bounced, a ridiculous snake of curves and coils. They hopped to the edge, and stood again in a line, arms up and hands resting on each other's shoulders.

The Fat Girl looked down at the ice, and through the moonglow, she could see movement beneath the crust. The water was there, the waves were there, waiting to offer the embrace. They only had to dip their toes in. Only their toes.

"Use your heels and crack the ice!" the Fat Girl called.

Bare heels, a flash of brown and pink and almond, plummeted down and the sound of the ice when it broke was like thunder. The Fat Girl felt lightning freeze up her foot to her knee and on to her thigh, and she knew by the shrieks around her that the others were zapped too. Then they stood there, their heels dripping, and they watched the jagged line of ice sweep forward, move back, sweep forward, with the force of the released waves.

"Okay," the Fat Girl said. "Okay, let's just dip our toes in. Just our toes. Ready? On the count of three."

The Fat Girls pointed their toes, suddenly ballerinas, and they stood there, poised, pointed, ready, in the moonlight. The water waited.

One.

Two.

Three.

Ever so gently, the Fat Girls dipped their toes in. They held them there, the water gracing around them, and they stood, arm in arm in arm, their faces upraised to the moon. To the grand tiara. They were bathed in silver, in the air, on their faces, down their bodies, to their toes, lightly in the moonshine water. The Fat Girl felt the shiver, but also the warm embrace of the woman next to her.

For a moment, the Fat Girl's thoughts flitted to the finalists of that night's beauty pageant. The way those women stood there, smiles fixed and perfect, in their ball gowns, their arms around each other, but staring straight ahead at the audience. At the cameras. Their arms were loose and if one had stepped away, they would have all remained standing. Not like this. Not like here. Here, the Fat Girl knew, if an arm went down, they would all wobble, then hit the dirt. The Fat Girl shoved the States away, replaced her vision instead with this group of fifteen, and behind them, all the customers, standing in line through the store and filling the fitting rooms, eating warm cookies, drinking hot coffee, and laughing and cheering each other on. Cheering each other on!

The Fat Girl looked down the line, at the row of fifteen delicately placed feet. They had their toes in the water. Yes, they did. All of their toes were in the water.

SUNDAY

The seventh angel poured out his bowl into the air, and out of the temple came a loud voice from the throne, saying, "It is done!"

During the holiday season, the mall closed late, at ten o'clock, even on weekends. The manager showed up on this Sunday at nine-thirty and she knew the others were surprised to see her. She wasn't supposed to work weekends, she was the manager, but yesterday, Saturday, she'd come in anyway and it was wonderful. While some retailers grumped about the holiday season, claiming the crowds were nasty and rude and impatient, the manager found it to be the exact opposite. There were some bad customers, of course, but the majority at Large & Luscious seemed to breathe a sigh of relief when they entered these doors. The manager was sure that it had something to do with how she and her employees genuinely liked each other, and they liked their customers too and that feeling just somehow spread to the store walls and floor and clothing. The customers' personalities erupted when they tried on Large & Luscious clothes. If they walked in sad, they walked out happy. If they walked in happy, they walked out happier.

It was always easy to see a first-time Large & Luscious customer. She often passed by the entrance several times, obvious in her need to be hidden, waiting for a lull in the mall crowd. Then she skulked in, glancing behind her, her body curved forward, like a turtle in its shell. When the greeter at the counter smiled at her and called a welcome, the new customer ducked and made a run for the store's perimeter. Moving around cautiously, each footstep carefully placed, she clutched her purse and her eyes darted everywhere, taking in all of the colors, all of the fabrics. The first thing to relax would be her shoulders. She would start paging through the clothes, choosing a few here and there, and then more and more. By the time she asked for a dressing room, her cheeks would be flushed with excitement, her arms laden. Someone in the fitting area, either a clerk or another customer, would start a conversation and soon words volleyed back and forth and clothing choices and stories were shared. At the cash register, all would be smiles and enthusiasm. And then, right before leaving, the new customer would carefully tuck her pink bag under a coat. She hovered for a moment, just inside and to the right or left of the doors. After looking both ways, she slipped out as if she was hiding a good secret. Or maybe not, but the manager liked to tell herself that. Either way, by the customer's third visit, she would stride in, choose her clothes with exhilaration and expectation, and then leave with the pink bag fully in sight. In fact, usually two or more bags.

The manager just loved it. Really. Some people threw the word love around like onion powder, adding just a pinch of flavor to every recipe. I love that dress. I love those flowers. I love the color green. I love that movie. But the manager, when she said she loved her store, meant it. All the way down to her bones. Through all of her many layers to her blood. To whatever it was that made the manager the manager. Whatever it was that made her a Fat Girl.

Especially on Sundays, the manager felt the need to stop in. She checked on her store, checked on her girls, but really, she just wanted to sit and wait for the next week to kick in. On the calendar, the manager knew that the week started with Sunday. But in her life, in her store, the week ended with Sunday and on Monday, it all started over again.

The manager double-checked the register tape and then sent one of the Fat Girls off with the deposit. She said goodnight to the others and told them she wanted to do a few things before Monday's opening. When the Fat Girls finally left, the manager slid the glass doors closed, locked them, and turned on the security lights.

The clothes glowed dimly, setting up the impression of hundreds of candles placed throughout the room. Just outside the fitting area, there were a couple easy chairs and a bench, for those waiting for customers inside, or for those waiting for a fitting room to be free. The manager always chose the center chair, big and soft, and close enough to the bench to use it as a footrest. From there, she knew, the security guard on patrol would never see her, and she could just sit and look and enjoy what was hers. Without being embarrassed. Without being judged.

This was her store.

Well, not hers, of course, not exactly; she didn't own it. But she managed it, she was the Fat Girl in charge of the Fat Girls, and no matter who actually owned it, it was her domain. Once, there'd been a break-in late at night, and when the security guard called her, to let her know the wanna-be thief was already caught and there weren't any damages beyond broken glass in the door and a mutilated cash register, and there wasn't any need for her to come in until morning, the manager got up anyway, threw on a coat, and drove to the mall. The store was as he said, broken glass adding an evil leer to the manager's newly vacuumed carpet, a twisted and wrenched cash drawer where the culprit found no cash anyway, and a few outfits tossed like body outlines on the floor. The manager felt bruised. She checked the tossed clothes carefully, found no rips, and hung them back in place. Then she went through all of the racks, determining the health of each garment, examined each mannequin, made sure the jewelry was still free of tangles. The fitting rooms were clean, the security lights lit. By the time she left, the morning girls were on their way in, and the security guard had put plywood up over the broken door and swept up all the shards of glass. The wound would be slid away, out of sight of the customers. When the Fat Girls asked the manager what happened, she cried. It was almost the only time the manager cried in front of her girls.

Almost. There'd been cancer for one Fat Girl. A horrible accident for another.

Sitting there, the store so silent without its piped music, without the voices of the customers and the Fat Girls, the manager thought of those girls gone missing, and her once-battered store, and she felt tears well up again. But then she pushed them away.

It was just life, she knew. These things happened to everyone. And still, her life was full. At the end of every Sunday, she was grateful. There was always the store, there were always her girls, and there were always the customers. She felt responsible for them all; and that responsibility was like joy.

Sometimes, if she was there in the morning, before the doors opened, the manager felt like they were in a fishbowl. The mall walkers cruised by outside, and many glanced in. Some looked derisive, others fearful, and a few looked triumphant. It was like they were trying to run away from ever having to walk into Large & Luscious, from ever being with those inside. From ever being tainted. Branded. Sentenced to death.

But then, during the day, the doors were opened and the real world could come in, and the Fat Girls could go out. Sometimes, there was a happy comingling of the two. Mostly, though, there was the brazen walking in of returning customers, the shyness of the new, and the rest of the mall just turned their faces away. The manager wished sometimes that there weren't any walls between stores, no doors to the mall. That anyone who came in could find themselves anywhere; even here. There would be no division.

And at night, like this, tucked away in her chair, alone in her store, the manager just felt safe. Content. She protected the store; the store protected her. The rest of the world was locked outside. At night, segregation felt good. There were no voices to hear, no faces to see. No one to bolster, to encourage, and cheer. There was no need here. There was just the manager and the store. The manager felt her edges blur, and the store's edges blur. And they blended, the two of them. Partners. She couldn't explain it. But the store had a being all its own. On Sunday nights, when there was just silence and color and gentle light, the manager felt her hand held, her shoulders squeezed. The manager took care of everyone, but on Sunday nights, the store took care of her.

Standing up, the manager stretched, and the security guard, just passing by, startled. She laughed and waved and he smiled in return. After giving everything one more once-over, the manager slid the doors open, closed them, and locked them tightly.

"Late night tonight?" the security guard asked. Whenever they ran into each other, he and she had this same conversation. The manager knew it by heart.

"Just getting things settled," the manager said. "All's done. Ready for another week." She tried the doors again, one more time, and was happy with their snug fit.

"Goodnight now," she said, not knowing for sure whether she meant the security guard or the store; well, really, she did, but she nodded at the guard anyway. Turning, the manager headed for the exit, keeping the store's key firmly tucked in the palm of her hand.

GOD, ADAM, EVE, AND WOMAN, AS TOLD BY THE FAT GIRL

A Poem

They say that Adam was made in God's image, and I believe it, she says, and that God's a man. Because only a man would make a man tall, blond and ripped, with a dick so large, it had to be covered by the leaf of the ficus lyrata to make him modest, and to keep Adam from fiddling with himself.

And true to form, she belly-laughs.

And when Adam whined that he needed to fiddle, and God figured fiddling was sinful (self-abuse), He reached into Adam's stomach (the way to a man is through his stomach) and plucked Himself a rib. Thin and curved. God awarded Adam with boners in exchange for his sacrifice and then God waved His wand (it ain't the size of the wand, remember, but the magic, though I think one can assume God's is both big and magical; he's God, she says) and there was Eve. Born of Adam's rib and God's wand. She was tall, blonde and built, with boobs huge and bare; who cared about modesty there, expose the jugs, and He hid her bush with another leaf. How the hell do you hide a bush with a leaf? If a tree falls in the forest, does it make a sound?

You figure it out, she says.

Well, at least this is what the artists depict, and given our history, it makes sense. Artists are known for the truth. Well, sometimes. Look at David and Venus di Milo. So Eve, by Adam's desire and maybe God's own, didn't have a brain, but she did have an appetite, though it wasn't necessarily for Adam's dick. Eve hungered for something big and red and crunchy, and well, you just don't get that giving head. Much. So Eve was hungry for something she didn't have, and she ate the apple and you know the rest. If it was left to Eve, and Adam, and God, Womanhood would be damned for all eternity.

Funny , she says, that a bone-skinny woman would be cursed for eating something healthy.

But see, then Woman had a taste. She learned Delicious. Woman kept the rib, but began to pack the meat on. Blonde, hungry, little-brain Eve took her appetite and her fig leaf and her jugs and propagated and Amazons cracked out of her eggs. They prowled through the 14th century, larger than life, larger than love, larger than an apple, and they grew and they felt their size. They felt their voices. They found their power. They fought in wars. And won.

And yeah, she says, Amazons cut off one breast. The better to fit their weapons. They had to learn to deal with their own roundness. And learn the weapon that
was theirs. Then they grew 'em back.

Before the 14th C turned to the 15th, Amazons burst out voluptuous, and the word Voluptuous was born. It meant full of pleasure. Pleasure! she says. Because Men began to grow too and slid their eyes from the Eves of the world and ran their gazes up, down, over, around and under the Amazons. Sized them up. Full of pleasure. Just bursting.

You just gotta bust what's bursting, she says. You just gotta touch.

In the 15th century, Voluptuous was tagged as Addiction. Addiction to "sensual pleasure." Hooked on Fornication! It doesn't take even a brain the size of Eve's to figure what happened there. Men, Women, Amazons, more cushion, less pushin', luxury, lavish, buffet, grab a big breast here, grab a fat ass there, and oh, baby, baby, feel the ground move! Feel it howl and rumble!

And roar! she says.

In the 16th century, Peter Paul Rubens arrived, and so did his ladies in their altogether and folks lined up to stare, she says. Like the cat that ate the canary. Like the man that ate the woman and the woman that ate the man and they ate together out of the raw bounty this world has to offer. Some said the word Rubenesque like it was a bad taste in their mouths, but some let it roll around their tongues and their teeth and they pooched out their cheeks and you just know there was Feasting going on. Finger-lickin Feasting with saliva and semen and salty juices galore. In the art studio. Behind the galleries. In rooms everywhere. You can bet these weren't titters from teeny tiny tits, but the raucous from outrageous breadths. Powerful, like Amazons. Appetite, like Eve. And Sensual from one roll to the next on a curvy couch of a body that just sunk Man's ass in. And his dick too, from behind the ficus.

Enlarged Hearts

They fiddled, she says, and giggles.

Somehow, in the 30's, the word Zaftig appeared, sounding ominous and Nazi and harsh. Yet it was the Jews that created it, the Jews that erupted it, and it meant juicy and succulent and Woman. Woman! A Zaftig Woman was a Rubenesque Woman, an Amazon of fulfilling desires. And Voluptuous cavorted with Webster the Second and birthed sensual pleasure and feminine beauty combined. Connected. One.

Feminine beauty, she says. And places a hand gently on her bust.

So a Voluptuous Woman is a beautiful Woman. And a Voluptuous Woman is a Zaftig Woman. And a Zaftig Woman is a Rubenesque Woman. And a Rubinesque Woman is an Amazon, borne straight out of Eve's slender thighs. We've come a long way since an apple in the garden.

A long way since God and His image, she says.

Did God create us? Not even close. He made a Xerox of His image and then Eve from a rib bone for Man and his ficus lyrata. Woman made Woman, hungering hard from Eve's appetite and forming bodies thick with our souls. With our voices and our strengths and our desires.

God and His image be damned. It took a Fat Girl to set this world straight, she says.

Hallelujah. And Amen.